D1453280

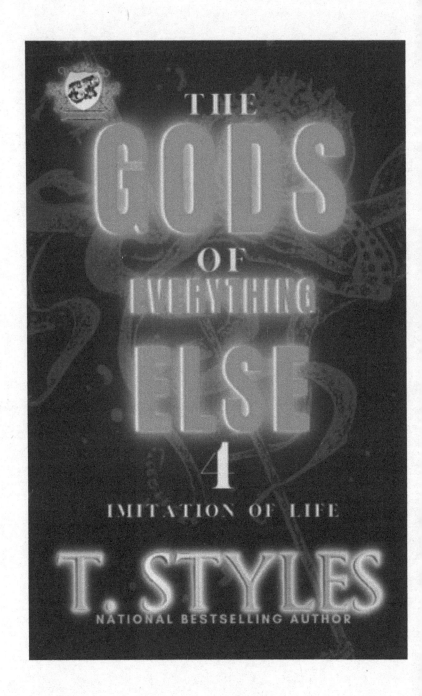

THE
GODS
OF
EVERYTHING
ELSE
4
IMITATION OF LIFE

T. STYLES

NATIONAL BESTSELLING AUTHOR

By T. STYLES

ARE YOU ON OUR EMAIL LIST?

SIGN UP ON OUR WEBSITE

www.thecartelpublications.com

SHYT LIST 1: BE CAREFUL WHO YOU CROSS
SHYT LIST 2: LOOSE CANNON
SHYT LIST 3: AND A CHILD SHALL LEAVE THEM
SHYT LIST 4: CHILDREN OF THE WRONGED
SHYT LIST 5: SMOKIN' CRAZIES THE FINALE'
PITBULLS IN A SKIRT 1
PITBULLS IN A SKIRT 2
PITBULLS IN A SKIRT 3: THE RISE OF LIL C
PITBULLS IN A SKIRT 4: KILLER KLAN
PITBULLS IN A SKIRT 5: THE FALL FROM GRACE
POISON 1
POISON 2
VICTORIA'S SECRET
HELL RAZOR HONEYS 1
HELL RAZOR HONEYS 2
BLACK AND UGLY
BLACK AND UGLY AS EVER
MISS WAYNE & THE QUEENS OF DC
BLACK AND THE UGLIEST
A HUSTLER'S SON
A HUSTLER'S SON 2
THE FACE THAT LAUNCHED A THOUSAND BULLETS
YEAR OF THE CRACKMOM
THE UNUSUAL SUSPECTS
LA FAMILIA DIVIDED
RAUNCHY
RAUNCHY 2: MAD'S LOVE
RAUNCHY 3: JAYDEN'S PASSION
MAD MAXXX: CHILDREN OF THE CATACOMBS (EXTRA RAUNCHY)
KALI: RAUNCHY RELIVED: THE MILLER FAMILY
REVERSED
QUITA'S DAYSCARE CENTER
QUITA'S DAYSCARE CENTER 2
DEAD HEADS
DRUNK & HOT GIRLS
PRETTY KINGS
PRETTY KINGS 2: SCARLETT'S FEVER
PRETTY KINGS 3: DENIM'S BLUES
PRETTY KINGS 4: RACE'S RAGE
HERSBAND MATERIAL
UPSCALE KITTENS
WAKE & BAKE BOYS
YOUNG & DUMB
YOUNG & DUMB: VYCE'S GETBACK
TRANNY 911
TRANNY 911: DIXIE'S RISE
FIRST COMES LOVE, THEN COMES MURDER
LUXURY TAX
THE LYING KING
CRAZY KIND OF LOVE
SILENCE OF THE NINE
SILENCE OF THE NINE II: LET THERE BE BLOOD

4

By T. STYLES

WWW.THECARTELPUBLICATIONS.COM

THE GODS OF EVERYTHING ELSE 4   5

THE GODS OF EVERYTHING ELSE 4: IMITATION OF LIFE

By

T. STYLES

Library of Congress Control Number: 2021925342

ISBN 10: 1948373920

ISBN 13: 978-1948373920

Cover Design: Book Slut Girl

First Edition

Printed in the United States of America

What's Up Famo,

I hope this letter/love note finds y'all in good health and happiness. If not, go and do something to make you smile! It's already July 2023 and before you know it, it'll be Christmas. Don't waste time on things that don't matter. As my baby always says, give yourself grace, take care of you today!

Now, onto the prized possession in your hands...**THE GODS OF EVERYTHING ELSE 4**! This next installment in the Wales & Louisville ongoing epic family saga did NOT disappoint! I read it in one sitting and once you crack it open, I know you will get just as pulled in! Book 16 in this series just proves that T. Styles is a creative mastermind and I'm here for it all!

Now, let's shift our focus and keep in line with tradition. In this novel, we want to give a well-deserved shout out to our son:

JUAN AKA "REEKO KING"

By T. STYLES

Juan is not only our son, but a phenomenal actor! He's been working for the family business since he was fourteen years old and has been in almost every last one of our movie projects. Recently, Juan has stepped into leading roles and has been knocking them out the park! Having acting credits in over eight movies, he's a veteran in this game with more exciting roles coming soon. We couldn't be prouder of him! Make sure you check him out as leading man, **COLIN** in, *"I'M HOME"*, streaming currently on Amazon and Tubi. Also, check him out as, **KELSI** in our upcoming movie, *"A HUSTLER'S SON",* releasing this summer!

Aight, I've kept you from this masterpiece long enough, grab your favorite snack and beverage, hunker down in a comfortable chair or bed, and get to it!

Love and Light to you always!

C. Wash

Vice President

The Cartel Publications

www.thecartelpublications.com

www.facebook.com/authortstyles

www.facebook.com/Publishercwash

Instagram: Publishercwash

Instagram: Authortstyles

www.twitter.com/cartelbooks

www.facebook.com/cartelpublications

www.theelitewritersacademy.com

Follow us on IG: Cartelpublications

Follow our Movies on IG: Cartelurbancinema

#CartelPublications

#UrbanFiction

#PrayForCece

#ReekoKing

#THEGODSOFEVERYTHINGELSE4

By T. STYLES

PROLOGUE

"We looking good!" The Belizean pilot boasted from the cockpit. "Clear skies the entire ride!"

As if it ruled the air, the sexy black private jet soared, its sleek exterior reflecting the yellow hues of the setting sun. The word WALES in silver plastered across both sides let the lessers know which billionaire owned the world.

Of course it was Banks Wales!

Or so they thought.

Playing the role of Banks, Ace Wales, a man of mystery and charm, reclined in the cocaine white plush leather seat, his tailored black suit accentuating his impeccable style. The smoked colored 24k gold shades made it difficult to see he was on his imposter shit, because his eyes were hidden behind expensive ombre lenses.

By his side, his breathtakingly beautiful woman, Arbella was propped and ready for show. Sure she wasn't Banks' wife, Faye Wales. But what wealthy man you knew didn't have a little something younger on the side? Her long flowing hair cascading downward like a black waterfall around her delicate chocolate features made her look unreal.

She was bad for sure and yet her eyes laid heavy with the troubles of this trip. But she had better not show it because her fear, her worry, could ruin it all.

They were entertaining two bankers, hoping that they would buy what Ace was selling and do what he wanted. To transfer all money and assets from Banks to his son, Ace Wales.

Yep, for the evening Ace had taken over his father's persona and Arbella was a willing and sexy accomplice. The bankers legit assumed that it was the king who was taking the meeting because Ace was back on his old shit.

Greed.

Treachery.

Deceit.

To his family, he had proven that he would forever be a monster who would do everything he could to not only live like his father but become his father.

And yet something felt off to the guests.

In the spacious cabin, Mr. Blackwood and Mr. Harrington nervously exchanged glances at one

By T. STYLES

another. They had met Mr. Wales briefly only two other times in person, so they were somewhat confused. Normally Faye conducted all business face to face. Because Banks couldn't be bothered. He was running too many businesses. He would simply log on and see that what he expected was reflected in his banking accounts.

Each time it was.

So this was different.

Still, if the man before them was the great Banks Wales, who was up in age, the years did him well. Like he could bottle what he was taking because he looked so fucking good.

Don't get it twisted.

Ace moved like Banks.

Sounded like Banks.

But he was not Banks.

He practiced for months before making the switch. And since he was his son, the features he possessed made it easier for those to believe who wanted to believe the lie. He even went all out to have gray hair that was kept in a low curly $300 haircut. But where were the wrinkles? Where were the soft crinkling of the skin on the hands that indicated age had visited and within near time death would follow?

"So I expect you have everything you need to transfer my funds to my son when it's time?" Ace said in his best daddy 'War-Banks' voice. "Like I mentioned I haven't been feeling well and I want to ensure all funds are in order if anything happens to me."

"Of course," Mr. Blackwood nodded. "Although we're unsure why you wouldn't get your lawyers involved."

"Mainly because they handle things when I'm dead." He took a sip and dusted invisible lint off his clothes. "But as you both can see, a nigga is still alive."

They cleared their throats.

"We understand," Mr. Blackwood said. "And I know you're upset about all of the hoops we made you jump through. But we needed to make sure you know..."

"No, I don't know."

"What my colleague is saying is that...well...you are leaving billions to him. Not to mention you just made a huge transfer to Mason Louisville. So we want to make sure that you are...well."

Earlier that month to make sure Mason knew that he cared for him and his legacy, Banks broke off half of his funds to him. That was done with

By T. STYLES

paperwork and lawyers. But when "fake Banks" wanted to do it again so soon, the bankers sounded off an alert.

And this is what sponsored the charade in the jet.

"Well, are you satisfied now?" Ace said. "That I want my wishes carried out?"

The silence was heavy.

In it held a lot. Would all benefit from the blue-sky robbery that was obviously taking place by siphoning tons under the guise of Ace being his father?

"We are satisfied," Blackwood said with a slight smile.

"Good." Ace said, on his best boss shit. "And don't worry. All of my future funds will continue to go through Blackwood & Harrington Bank. With the deal I'm closing now, it will make your institution one of the wealthiest in the world."

As the jet cruised at a dizzying altitude, suddenly Ace's focus shifted from the men to the unsettling noises coming from the cockpit. The plane rattled, the engine sputtered, and alarms blared. A growing sense of trepidation settled over the passengers as they realized something was gravely wrong.

They were falling.

Fast!

Flying back and forth like a ball in a foosball game, Ace rose and rushed into the cockpit.

What he saw next caused his heart to rattle.

The pilot was slumped forward, and he was both unconscious and unresponsive as he shook him for dear life. "Johnson, get up! Wake the fuck up!"

He didn't.

Slowly Ace backed up in fear.

"What's wrong with the pilot?" Blackwood said standing behind him. He hadn't even known he was there.

Ace looked back at him. "I...I don't know!"

"Well you're a pilot, right?!" He yelled. "What are you waiting on? Fly us to safety!"

CHAPTER ONE
12 DAYS EARLIER

Earlier that day due to a fire that consumed their mansion and surrounding land, Banks had taken his family to a luxury hotel only to learn that he was the initial warden that would ultimately keep him and his entire family hostage.

But for the moment no one was aware. Besides, it was a beautiful place of refuge. The floor to ceiling windows sparkled as Banks took in the beauty of Belize.

It wasn't Wales Island, but it would do.

The moon shone over the ocean causing it to glow in the distance. The dancing trees brought Banks a serenity that he didn't know he needed in that moment.

Turning around he looked at Mason, Spacey, Minnesota, and Joey and tried to be confident, which is what they needed at that moment. They were worried and waited for him to say something great. After all, Banks always had an answer.

Did he have one now?

"We are entering a new chapter. And we are going to have to work hard to keep each other strong."

"Agreed," Mason said firmly. "But we can–."

Suddenly the door opened, and Ace entered with Arbella and six armed men. Their first order of duty was putting a bullet into Banks' most loyal guard. Paulo fired right into his gut. He dropped on the floor. And as they looked at his blood pour from his body Banks trembled with rage.

In fear Minnesota said, "He looks like pops." She was referring to Ace. "Moving like him too. What the fuck?"

"This nigga just won't die," Spacey said throwing his hands up.

"Hey, brother," Ace grinned.

"Fuck do you want with us now, nigga?" Spacey yelled. "Just leave us the fuck alone! Damn!"

Ace's men stepped in front of his family members, with weapons aimed in their direction. "You'll find out soon enough." He paused and nodded at his men who removed hoods from their pockets. "Everybody on the floor! Now!"

They obeyed, backs against the open window.

Banks said, "My men will come in this–."

"My men." Ace corrected. "The nigga we dropped was the only one who chose to stay loyal. Look at where that got him." Banks was heated.

Mason had tried to warn him that Ace was up to something evil earlier that week, but Banks didn't listen. Now it was too late.

"Don't do this, son," Mason begged. "There is still time to turn things around. Reconnect with family."

"But if you do this, whatever this is, it's done," Banks said firmly. "And you will not win."

For a second Ace looked at his family sitting on the living room floor, mostly afraid for their lives. Something moved in the pit of his stomach at that moment. Was this the right thing?

Because if he made a move, it would be like drawing a blood line in the sand. One he couldn't come back from.

"This nigga don't give a fuck about us," Spacey said, breaking Ace's thought process. "He can suck my dick for all I care."

Mason, knowing Ace was possibly coming around, shook his head. "You should have stayed quiet, Spacey." He whispered, realizing he fucked up. There was a moment of humanity in his son, but his brother ruined it all.

Ace nodded to his men to move closer with the bags for their heads.

"So you're just gonna kidnap a whole billion-dollar family?" Banks asked. "Kidnapping? You're adults. This a straight up snatching!"

Within seconds all of their heads were covered with satchels, snuffing out the moonlight.

Banks and his family had been taken hostage...

And once again Banks realized his own son was involved. If you knew the history of the Wales family, surely you'd remember how Banks killed Jersey, the woman who used her body to give Ace and Walid life.

The woman who was first Mason's wife...

And second, Banks'...

This same woman, due to street politics and beyond, Banks killed. Justifiably or not, who cares. At the end of the day her death meant she was not in a position to flood the twins, Ace in particular, with a womanly gaze necessary to prevent men from turning into monsters.

And so Ace was wildin' out in the worst way possible.

And this was the beginning.

The next morning the satchels were taken off of Banks, Mason, Spacey, Minnesota, Joey, and Blakeslee's heads by an extra-large Belizean man with a stained black shirt, greasy hair, and strong gaze. Behind him was Paulo, Ace's goon who smiled as the beast tore off the covers on their heads as if he were trying to rip their scalps off.

As they blinked to see clearly through the brightness, Banks said, "Where are the boys?" He was calm but assertive.

"And where is Sugar?" Minnesota questioned, even though the child was Blakeslee's birth daughter.

The boys, better known as the Triad, consisted of 15-year-old Patrick, who was Mason's grandson, 14-year-old Bolt, who was Mason's son and 16-year-old Riot, who was Spacey's only child.

"Ace wants me to let you know that they are well. Sugar is with them, enjoying her time in this beautiful hotel," He grinned. "No harm will come to them, although I can't say the same about you."

Mason glared.

"But I am Paulo." A firm hand sat above his heart, next to his throat and Banks wished he'd choke himself out. "And I'm in charge."

"Do you know who I am?" Banks said firmly but with much power. "Do you really know?"

"That is not the question...the question is, do you know Paulo?"

"What you doing here is dangerous," Mason said.

"Are you threatening me?"

"It's a statement, not a threat," Spacey said.

The moment he opened his mouth Banks and the gang cringed. Spacey had a knack of rubbing niggas the wrong way, and no one was quite sure why.

Paulo smiled and began to pace in front of them while they sat on the floor. Their lower backs in pain due to being propped on the hard ceramic all night. "You are rich, but with all of your money, you aren't smart enough to know when you are not in charge. And that attitude, if it doesn't change, will cause you your life."

"You can tell when a nigga never had power," Spacey said, shaking his head with a smirk on his face. "Fucking cornball."

24   **By T. STYLES**

Paulo stopped in front of him and smiled.

Next he stole him in the face, whipping his head to the left. Spacey's entire mouth flooded with blood.

Teeth ran pink.

Mason, Joey and even Minnesota, wanted at him so badly, they attempted to wiggle out of the ropes which tied their arms behind their backs, but the goon was on them and ready.

Banks remained still, observing the beast. "Steady yourselves, family." Banks warned. "Steady." He would see him brought to his knees so help him God, but now was not the time.

"Fuck is wrong with you?" Mason yelled at Paulo. "Was that fucking necessary?"

Paulo laughed, turned back, and nodded at the man at the door. The larger man walked out, brought in trays filled with light food. Toast. Boiled eggs. Water. Next he brought in another tray loaded with fresh fruit, coffee, steak, and eggs.

"This one is everyone else's," Paulo said, pointing to the lesser breakfast. "This one is for you," he pointed at Banks. He paused. "If anyone but you eats this, I will pump a bullet in the same mouth," he said pointing at Spacey.

Banks gritted his jaw.

The threats against his family rubbed him all kinds of wrong but again he remained calm. At the same time if he knew who he was, he would have never leveled such threats.

"Do you understand?" He asked Banks.

"All things."

Paulo smiled and the ropes were released from their arms. "You may also go to that bathroom. We will remain outside this room in case one of you wants to meet the lord a bit sooner."

With that he exited, leaving them alone.

Rubbing his wrist Mason looked down at Spacey and said, "You just can't shut the fuck up, can you?"

"I mean for real," Joey said as he moved toward the bathroom. "Now look at your shit! All bloodied up."

As the others got up, stretched, and talked about what went down, Banks remained still in contemplation.

This would be his biggest test.

He knew it.

By T. STYLES

CHAPTER TWO

Walid and Aliyah walked toward a turquoise-colored house as the sun casted a warm glow upon their faces. In the city, melodic sounds of Kriol music drifted in the air while smells greeted their senses, embracing them in the warmth of Belizean hospitality.

Earlier that day Baltimore Wales – Walid, and Aliyah's son, had been dropped off to a bonded caregiver as well as three armed guards to ensure he would be okay. Because for what was about to go down, he needed his son protected.

War was in the midst.

As they continued walking Walid replayed the call he had received from a stranger. *"It's a friend of the family. I can't give you my name. I want you to know you do not want to come to the resort. Your family is being held hostage by Ace and his men. They need help. I'll reach back out when I can. Just know you have an ally."*

The call never came.

And after checking resorts and not seeing their vehicles he reasoned Ace had taken them to some place less visible.

But where?

As they walked up to the house, Aliyah knocked once, and the door opened. A small boy no more than five-years-old opened the door and said, "Come! Come in!"

After he let them in, he disappeared and reappeared again.

Walid and Aliyah smiled at his energy and noticed how the interior of the home exuded a charming rustic style with its weathered wooden furniture and vibrant tapestry hanging on the walls.

Soft rays of sunlight filtered through the windows, emitting playful patterns on the worn terracotta floor tiles.

"This way," the kid said happily. "She's in the kitchen!"

Again they followed and the tantalizing scent of freshly ground spices, mingling with the rich aroma of simmering stews and the gentle sweetness of tropical fruits, filled their nostrils, creating a symphony of flavors that danced in the air.

In the heart of the kitchen stood a woman, her hands skillfully moving through the meal. Her eyes sparkled with a warmth that mirrored the home's inviting atmosphere and her caramel-colored skin glowed in the soft light.

"Hey, Tia," Aliyah said to her aunt.

"Have a seat."

She was both nice and short at the same time, which fucked Walid up. Was she friend or foe? The verdict was not in.

They pulled wooden chairs away from the table and sat and waited. It was obvious that this was her show.

Her hair, adorned with a vibrant floral scarf, framed her face like a work of art. Originally from Brazil, Aliyah's aunt always infused her home country into her everyday life.

With graceful movements, she set a table with a traditional feijoada simmered in a large clay pot. Its aroma of slow-cooked black beans, smoked meats, and spices filled the room with an irresistible allure.

Beside it, bowls of farofa, a toasted cassava flour dish, and crispy kale chips. Freshly squeezed passion fruit juice glistened in glasses, inviting Walid and Aliyah to quench their thirst.

But neither touched shit because something felt off.

The woman approached them with an open-hearted hospitality, her voice filled with warmth and love.

But Walid saw something else. "This is a lot of food."

Aliyah, doing her best to relax his mind, said, "My auntie always cooks a lot. You never know if—"

"Who else is coming over here?" He asked the older woman. "Who else are you expecting?" His energy was guarded and serious.

"The boy king, in the flesh." A male voice called out from behind.

When Walid turned around, he saw a familiar face and got his answer. She was cooking for the enemy.

Many years ago, before Walid met Aliyah, Ace had gotten into trouble during a game of soccer with Dominik and his boys. That exact game ended in a chase with Walid coming to the rescue and getting his brother out of the village of Gales. What's worse, that same event ended in the death of Aliyah's father who was struck with Walid's

By T. STYLES

vehicle by accident. A secret she hadn't known until recently which tore her and Walid apart.

"Dominik, what are you doing here?" Aliyah asked, her heart pounding out of her chest. She rose to her feet. "Tia, what's going on?" She asked her aunt. "What are you doing?"

"There is unfinished business." Her aunt said viciously. "This man drove a car which killed your father! My brother!" She pointed at Walid. "And you bring him here for help? To my home!" Her fingers trembled over her heart. "How dare you, Aliyah! How dare you!"

"But he didn't mean to, Tia! He..."

Walid placed a steady hand on Aliyah's shoulder. "It's okay."

Suddenly six more men stood behind Dominik in the kitchen doorway.

"I'll be fine." Walid said again.

Aliyah quivered, her teeth chattering from fear's icy grip. "Walid, I...I don't know about this. There are so many of them and–."

"Easy, baby," he said calmly. It was the first time he'd shown genuine love and concern to her since they had broken up many years ago. "Easy." He turned to Dominik. "What you wanna do, nigga?"

"Finish what your brother started." Dominik said, cracking his knuckles.

"Let's do it."

"Walid, please don't go out there. I'm afraid you—."

He grabbed Aliyah with one arm around her waist and whispered in her ear. Her body felt like a board against his own. "I'm supposed to help my family. I'm supposed to be there for my son. That means I'm protected by a higher Being. No matter what happens to me, it won't be permanent. I will see Baltimore become a man, so help me God."

Her body softened.

She believed him.

"Let's get it over with." He followed Dominik and the fellas outside to the back of the house.

Dominik immediately removed his shirt, showing his older but still muscular frame. Walid felt no need to remove his garbs. Instead he took the position of a boxer ready for the title match.

Dominik's men made a circle around the group while Aliyah and her aunt stood in the background, on the step and watched.

Dominik wasted no time and landed the first blow to Walid's face, and it was crushing. Back in the day, Walid was trained to fight, and he used to

By T. STYLES

roughhouse with his brother but in the current day billionaires were rarely struck about the face or body.

They didn't have to be.

Dominik tried to hit him again, but this time Walid moved and caught him with a punch that pushed him back into his friend Yazo's chest. He regained his footing.

Blow after blow ensued and one thing was clear.

When it came to matters of the street, Dominik had to fight and fight often so he had the upper hand. He understood the limits of his body as well as his power. And he was certain to make Walid feel it as his yellow skin cracked open with each blow, pouring blood onto his shirt.

This battle felt like it was to the death.

Suddenly they moved slower. The air not as full. Many minutes passed and before long it looked like it would be over, as Dominik threw one punch which knocked Walid to the clay-colored dirt.

But he got up, slowly and with tight fists in front of him, prepared for the next blow.

Dominik looked back at his men who long since stopped cheering. Walid was a fighter. Not a rich boy who wasn't prepared to back himself up. And so he quietly gained respect. From all who viewed the match.

Aliyah had covered her face in her Tia's breasts minutes earlier, so she had no idea how bad it had gotten. How much blood had poured. And if the love of her life was still breathing.

Or alive.

Looking at Walid who was wobbling, Dominik asked, "Why are you...why are you here?"

"I'm here to find my brother." He was out of breath. "I'm here to save my family, and I will die in this dirt trying."

He looked at one of his men who tossed him a towel. He tossed it to Walid. "You're looking for the one who looks like you right?"

Silence.

"Why you wanna find him?" Dominik continued.

He was dizzy. "I think he's going to...I think he may try to take over my father's life. And then I think he's gonna kill all of them."

Aliyah looked up at him because this was the first time she heard his thoughts.

"If he wants to be your father, maybe you should be glad." He chuckled. "Maybe your father is a better man than him."

"Anybody who says imitation is the greatest form of flattery never met an original nigga."

He laughed. "Tell me what you need. We'll help you find him. For now let's eat."

Relieved, Walid passed out.

CHAPTER THREE

Shit had fallen into line....

Ace had already secured the keys to his father's private jet which soared through the sky, its luxurious interior oozing opulence and sophistication. Ace reclined in the plush leather seat, his tailored navy-blue suit and fake gray hair accentuating his commanding presence.

By his side sat Arbella, her radiant beauty rivaling the sun's gentle caress.

But the lady in charge had penetrating eyes on another captivating woman onboard, Faye Wales, who despite being scared, emanated charm from every pore. It didn't help that she was once Ace's girl who later became Banks' wife.

At that moment, for sure she was Arbella's enemy.

As the jet cut through the clouds, Ace engaged in an intense conversation with Faye. Their words danced with the intricacies of business, negotiations, and the deal that waited to be sealed upon his arrival.

Because in order for Ace to take all.

By T. STYLES

He needed Faye's help.

There was literally no other way.

Of course Faye didn't want to assist Ace, but he had already kidnapped the entire Wales clan. What would stop him from throwing her out the plane if he so desired?

So she had to play the game, and she had to do it well.

"Are you sure this will work?" Ace said with a lowered gaze. "Because if I get the impression that you'll tell them who I really am, I will kill you."

"Haven't I already told you I'm willing to give you what you need?" She trembled. "Didn't I give you the info for the deal we're brokering today? Made sure the pilot let you hold the jet? Why you gotta threaten me every minute?"

"It's not a threat, it's a promise."

"What I'm telling you will seal the deal, Ace. I swear. And since you are going yourself, as Banks, you will be able to reroute the funds to the account we just set up. So you don't have to get his bankers involved." She took a deep breath. "At the same time it's up to you to convince them that you are Banks. I can't do that for you."

"I don't trust your ass." Arbella said, crossing her legs before whipping her hair over her shoulders.

"Fair."

Arbella glared.

"Fair? Bitch did you hear what I just said?"

"I did." She shrugged. "But what do you want me to say? It won't stop me from doing my job."

"Oh, so it's a job now?"

Silence.

"Answer me, whore!" Arbella was incensed and overcome with jealousy and rage.

"Look, I'm trying to save my life! And Banks' life!" She pointed at her heart. "So yes, I consider this to be a fucking job!"

"You a money hungry bitch." Arbella pointed at her. "And Banks should never have married your trifling ass. But you won't--."

"Go up front!" Ace said to Arbella.

"But she just--."

He raised up. "Now!"

She leapt up, stormed in the front, and shut the black curtain that separated the cabin, leaving them alone in the back. Ace took a deep breath and melted into the seat.

He was nervous about the upcoming meeting.

But Faye was ready.

She sat next to him and took a deep breath. It was obvious that she was fearful of the future but up for the challenge. "Ace, you're afraid."

Silence.

"It's not too late to stop this, Ace. It's not too late to--."

"My father will kill me if I don't go through with this now. There is no place I can go that will be safe. This must go down."

She sat next to him. Taking a deep breath she said, "You're agitated. You must be confident and easy if this is going to work. Banks doesn't have to tell people who he is. When he steps into a room, they know. They feel his power."

"I get it..."

"Do you really?" She leaned closer.

"Y...yeah."

"You're stiff. And that won't work." She sighed. "So what I'm about to do is not for you. It's about doing my part." Slowly she rose and eased between his legs.

"What you doing?" He shoved her back lightly on the shoulder.

She pressed forward. "You Banks or not?" She whispered. "Because if you're Banks, that makes me your wife. So let me help."

"But my girl will--."

"You don't have a girl. You have a woman. And I am your wife."

Removing his already stiffening dick from his pants she stroked it until it was so thick it throbbed between her fingertips. The fact that she was going down on him, coupled with the idea of getting caught, made him rock hard.

Low key he hated himself for it but what could he do?

Her mouth covered him like hot wax as her tongue played with the tip. In ecstasy he palmed the top of her head and eased in and out of her throat. He forgot how good she felt and suddenly he felt more like his father than his father ever could. After all, he had a dick and Banks was just "faking" to hear him tell it.

When it was all said and done, he exploded in her mouth and she cleaned every drop.

Wiping her plush lips with the back of her hand she took the seat Arbella once sat in across from him. "When this plane lands you will get that money. I will see to it...I promise."

By T. STYLES

He smiled. "You better, bitch."

She winked.

Banks, Mason, Spacey, Joey, Blakeslee and Minnesota sat around various places in the room.

Banks paced around as he worked out what could be going on in Ace's mind. What would be his next move and who could be helping him.

Agitated, Spacey tossed himself back on the bed. "This little nigga is up to--."

"That's your problem," Joey said, pointing in Spacey's direction. He stood off the floor and leaned on the wall. "You still think he a kid. And he done already showed niggas he ain't fucking around."

"You sound like a fan." Minnesota said, readjusting on the other side of the bed. The only mattress in the room. "He ain't doing nothing but getting on folks nerves."

"It ain't about that. What it's about is that we need to stop thinking he a kid and try to work out what he wants."

"I know what he wants. Money." Banks said, looking out the window. It was his favorite place. Without the window he would feel trapped. "He always wants money."

"Maybe...but he could've just asked. This feels more sinister." Mason added. He was seated on the chair by a desk.

"I think you're right," Blakeslee sat on the opposite side of the desk where Mason was, her bare toes spreading each time she swung her legs. "You're always sooo smart, Mason."

Spacey and Minnesota looked at one another. Because as of now, both of them were aware that she had fucked Mason. And they wanted to do everything in their power to prevent their father from finding out.

"If you not gonna contribute anything smart to say, stay quiet," Spacey said to Blakeslee.

"She's a part of this family," Banks announced. "She can speak if she wants to."

Blakeslee smiled and looked down. It was one of the few times Banks had taken up for her, but he was trying to do better with her feelings. Instead of blaming her for having his "dead name" which reminded him of his past.

But Minnesota and Spacey wanted the situation dealt with and when they got a chance, they would scare her again into secrecy. They knew she had fucked Mason and wanted him as her own. The girl was a helpless whore-matic, who had visions of running off with a person who could never be hers.

Quiet or not, the world knew that Banks and Mason were forever bonded, in ways that could not include Blakeslee. But she didn't care.

"Pops, all she's doing is agreeing with everything," Minnesota said. "I don't think that's contribution."

"It is to me."

"I gotta go to the bathroom," she said, sliding off the desk.

Quickly she rushed to the bathroom, closed the door, and pulled out the cell phone that was given to her last night by Ace. Because unlike the others, Ace still held a soft spot for his sister, so she was anything but a hostage.

He even told her, "You can come with me."

She simply said, "Nah. Let me be your eyes and ears."

And so he let her stay.

Dialing Ace's number she waited for him to answer. "What's wrong?" Ace said plainly on the other end.

She turned the water on to hide her words. "Nothing," she whispered, pacing the floor.

"Then call me later. I'm busy."

"I need a favor."

"What is it?"

"I wanna know if you gonna do it first."

"Tell me now or leave me the fuck alone. I got shit to do."

No one spoke in the room. Each was in their own world as if they knew something was about to happen. But one person knew things were about to change and her heart pumped hard every second.

Blakeslee sat nervously in the room with the crew while she watched the bedroom door impatiently. She focused on it so hard her eyes twitched, and her body trembled.

What was taking so long?

Suddenly the door flew open and Paulo and Big Greasy rushed inside. Bypassing everyone else, they grabbed Blakeslee and Mason as if they committed the worst crime.

"Fuck is going on?" Banks asked, finally losing control. "Where are you taking them?"

"Worry about yourself!" Paulo said, pointing in his face. "Like I told you before, you aren't in charge! You'd do well to remember that!"

With that he hustled both Blakeslee and Mason out of the room, leaving the rest confused.

Banks felt dizzy.

Spacey and Minnesota shook their heads while looking at one another.

While Joey rushed to his father's side.

Blakeslee, outside of their view, grinned.

Ace listened to her after all.

CHAPTER FOUR

A ce, Arbella, and Faye stood in the luxurious cherrywood mahogany elevator to ascend to the top of Plighton Industries.

Every now and again Ace would push his shades back, to ensure that his youthful eyes were hidden from view. After all, he was Banks Wales and had to keep the lie alive.

With each floor ascended, he felt more and more like he was out of his league.

DING.

The doors opened.

Arbella leaned over in his ear and said, "You will be fine. You got this." Next she looked over at Faye who hadn't even glanced her way. Besides, Faye wasn't new to this...she *was* this shit.

Feeling a little more powerful, they walked up to the boardroom where the door was immediately opened. After all, the occupants inside saw them on the camera.

The door opened and they strode into the palatial boardroom that reeked of power and wealth. The walls were adorned with masterful

By T. STYLES

works of art, and crystal chandeliers bathed the room in a warm glow, casting a money shine on the polished mahogany surfaces.

Around the table sat five young tech moguls, their faces a mix of anticipation and curiosity. They represented the future, the pioneers of innovation in a rapidly evolving world. While Ace, the master of deception, had positioned himself to seize an opportunity that would shape his destiny and put millions into his direct access.

After all, he had yet to get Banks to sign over the big money accounts. He hadn't even spoken to him about what exactly he wanted. So he needed this cash surge.

But he had a plan.

He had steps.

"This way," Stockton said, dressed in a white t-shirt and jeans. He pointed to three seats with their name cards on them.

This would be an unusual meeting for sure. Because Faye played her part seamlessly by being the embodiment of a supportive partner and confidante. While Arbella, Ace's real love, had assumed the role of an assistant, her beauty hidden behind a veil of professionalism.

This shit was crushing Arbella. All morning her eyes darted between Ace and Faye. She knew her nigga loved her but how far was he willing to go to be Banks Wales?

Would he cheat too?

As Ace approached the table, his confidence wavered for a moment. He dropped his briefcase, and a bead of perspiration formed on his forehead. Ole boy was about to fumble the bag and raise suspicions if he didn't get it together, that was certain.

But in that moment of vulnerability, Faye, the woman who had spent years by Banks' side, sensed his tension. And with a graceful ease, she stepped forward, her voice resonating with authority. "Gentlemen, allow me to introduce you to Banks Wales, the visionary who will guide us into a future defined by your groundbreaking innovation and our marketing."

The tech moguls leaned forward; their gazes fixed on Faye. She was better to look at anyway and they immediately found reassurance in her words. Besides, she was a tech boss in her own right, long before she met Banks, and this group of young men were her people.

A surge of adrenaline coursed through Ace's veins as she commanded the room and his heart pounded in his chest as he bet the house on her. He watched, almost in awe, as Faye seamlessly slipped into the role that he had concocted not even 48 hours ago.

With her at his side, the room seemed to shift in his favor and he had her to thank.

An hour later, Ace had relaxed and joined Faye in the performance while Arbella took frivolous notes to appear busy and less dumb.

"...coupled with our marketing department, we will ensure that Jiant Jestures becomes the most used app amongst your target audience. And we look forward to doing more business when this blows," Faye continued. "And it will blow."

"I can't lie," Stockton said. "This is what we're looking for from Wales Industries especially if you can follow through."

"He can follow through," Faye said, interrupting Ace before he could speak. "Besides, he's a genius." With that, Faye leaned in, her lips brushing against Ace's mouth in a gesture of affection. It was a calculated move, intended to solidify the charade of a happy husband and wife.

He kissed her back.

It also pissed the fuck out of Arbella.

Ace felt guilt and conflict because he hadn't told his girl that this would be a part of the plan.

He didn't even know.

Arbella was enraged. She was willing to endure the lies and manipulation, but this intimate moment between Ace and Faye pushed her to her breaking point threatening to destroy the plan.

"Well, gentlemen," Ace said, rising. "I hope we hear from you later today. We have left the paperwork with your attorneys. If everything looks to your liking, we expect the first transfer by the end of business tomorrow."

Stockton smiled. "Of course."

After hands were shaken, Ace, Faye and Arbella strutted out of the room. While Faye and Ace smiled at the mastery they just displayed, Arbella took the fuck off, leaving them alone as she moved toward the elevator.

"Is she okay?" Faye asked. "I didn't mean to kiss you and--."

He snatched her away from the camera. "You did mean to kiss me," he said through clenched teeth. "I'll take care of Arbella. You just make sure that you remember your place in this plan. You are not my woman. I don't care how much I let you suck my dick."

She nodded. "Of...of course. I'm sorry."

He released her and went after Arbella.

On the real, they were starting to piss Spacey off with the small ass meals. So the moment Big Greasy left, he said, "Fuck is going on? Why they feeding us like we rats?"

Banks, Spacey, Minnesota, and Joey sat huddled together in the dimly lit room, their bodies tense with fear and uncertainty. The meager breakfast before them provided zero solace, consisting of a couple of stale croissants and a lukewarm pot of coffee. While Banks' plate was filled with fresh fruit, soft bagels, and cream cheese.

"It's like they giving us bullshit but stuffing daddy up," Minnesota said. "Wait...you don't think they gonna eat him, do you?"

"Stop being dumb," Joey said. "This ain't no cannibalistic shit."

"At this point anything is on the table," Spacey admitted.

"I don't even want this shit." Joey bit down into one of the croissants. The tasteless morsels seemed to reflect the darkness of the situation. "I just hope this don't got no poison in it because..."

"What is this nigga doing?" Spacey said, throwing his hands up in the air. "I mean for real! Say what you want and leave us the fuck alone!"

"Which nigga you talking about?" Joey asked, chewing with his mouth open.

"Ace's ass!"

Minnesota rolled her eyes. "Trust me, I'm sure we all gonna find out what the fuck he got going on."

"You ain't lying about that," Joey said. "Soon too. Real soon."

Banks, his frustration mounting, slammed his hand against the wall. He walked over to the window and looked out before taking an angry deep breath. "Where the hell are Mason and Blakeslee? What did they do with them?"

"Then there's that," Joey said. "Why did he take them out of here?"

"We need fucking answers!" He yelled.

Banks had always been protective, fiercely guarding his family, and now, the uncertainty of their whereabouts messed with his soul. With all that said, he ain't let loose a mumbling word about his wife, Faye, and her mysterious absence.

Spacey, ever observant, and messy, nibbled on a dry croissant. "Pops, how come you ain't asking about Faye?"

Banks who was looking out the window turned to face him. "I...I don't...know. She was here with us, right?"

"Not since we first checked in last night," Joey said.

Banks walked away from the window. He desperately tried to replay in his mind the last time he saw her and sure as he was alive, he had forgotten all about shawty.

"You don't think nothing happened to her do you?" Minnesota asked.

"I don't...I...don't know," Banks whispered.

"Nah, Ace would have made it known." Spacey said. "Probably would've bragged on it like the bitch ass nigga that he is. I just don't know what he could be doing with her that's all."

"Then where the fuck is she?" Joey asked.

"You know I hate when niggas do that shit." Spacey said, pointing at him. "Asking questions but not contributing to the answer."

"That's all the fuck you do!" Joey snapped.

"Look, we don't know where she is right now." Banks said. "On my mind are the boys and Sugar, Mason, and Blakeslee. Faye can take care of herself. She always does."

Spacey and Minnesota looked at one another out of his view. Sure felt like he didn't give a fuck about her that was certain.

"Anyway, this little ass food ain't gonna do nothing but starve us to death," Joey said, interrupting the flow. "He probably wanna see that shit."

Slowly Minnesota and Spacey looked at each other again but this time as if they both saw the same ghost. And Banks and Joey caught their glances.

"What's wrong?" Banks asked.

"They...they *are* trying to starve us to death." Minnesota said, looking at Spacey.

After all, they were once starved by Banks' grandmother in the attic of her home. Before long, Minnesota was given food to survive, while Spacey was given little. Just like Banks was given more now. With that realization, they feared they were going through the same thing.

Again.

Together Minnesota and Spacey took the time to explain to Banks and Joey what may be happening. They gave more details of the ordeal with Banks' grandmother. And when they were done, everyone looked at the food on the table and agreed.

This was a death meal.

Banks took a deep breath.

Moving close enough so that only they could hear him he said, "Dig a hole in that wall. Put the stuff in there that can last for a while. Like the crackers and bread."

"Bread won't hold, Pops," Spacey said. "I've tried it before. One time I got sick."

"But it'll give us a few days." He responded. "We eat only when we can't take it anymore. We gotta preserve. And I'll come up with a plan."

"But he said we couldn't eat your food because–"

"There are no cameras in here," Banks said, glancing around. "I've looked at every inch of this room. The one camera that was in here is gone."

"What camera you talking about?" Joey frowned.

Minnesota smiled. "Blakeslee."

"Exactly," Banks winked.

By T. STYLES

CHAPTER FIVE

As the first rays of sunlight filtered through the windows of Aliyah's aunt's home, it put everything in a calming glaze. The living room, where everyone was posted up, was filled with plush sofas adorned in colorful throw pillows, and intricately patterned rugs gracing the polished wooden floor.

Seated around the table were Walid, Aliyah, Dominik, and Dominik's two male friends. The group of men and Aliyah may have looked picturesque, but shit was serious in that moment.

They shared a sense of urgency, made possible by Walid who was certain without real proof that Ace may be masquerading as their father only to kill everyone he loved once he got the bag.

Hours passed turning the day into the afternoon while the men exchanged theories and ideas about Ace's whereabouts based on his old ways. At one point Walid faded to the back as Dominik and his friends remembered all the times Ace came to town flaunting and showboating his father's money in an attempt to make the locals "feel poor".

Not one of them knew that he was the one really broke because he was searching for something even to the day he had yet to find and accept.

Love.

"I'll make more coffee," Tia said, placing a warm hand on her niece's shoulder.

Aliyah nodded and smiled and focused on her man and unlikely friends.

After another hour of nothingness, Walid stood up and walked to the window, just like his father. Nothing anyone was saying made sense. And the idea of losing his entire family did things to his mind he didn't think was possible.

While he excused himself, Dominik and his friends continued to talk all feeling as if they knew him better than his own twin.

"Ace likes his dick sucked," Walid said, looking out at the crowded town.

Everyone stopped talking and focused on Walid.

Aliyah looked for her aunt and then back at her man hoping she didn't hear him make such a crude statement. "Walid, what...what are you—."

By T. STYLES

"Before Arbella, before doing whatever the fuck this is he was doing, he liked his dick sucked."

Dominik shrugged. "So do all of us."

His friends nodded in agreement.

"But he likes it done not for the feeling. He likes it done for the power. So I don't know where he is, but if he remains in Belize, he will go to the places where he can feel in charge."

Dominik nodded. "I...I think you're right. He may be at a strip club."

"Nah," Walid shook his head.

"So you saying he won't be at a club or someplace like that?" Dominik's friend Yazo asked. "You're saying lower?"

"The in between," Walid stated.

"Where he can make a difference," Aliyah said.

"No...where he can feel the difference. Where a little bit of money can make the person he gives it to believe he's God. But he'll also want to shine."

"But Arbella is in the picture now," Aliyah said, wiping her hair out of her face. "I don't...I don't know if he's the same anymore."

"He's the same. Men like him don't change. I'm one hundred percent sure. Rich niggas have habits. And my brother is no exception."

CHAPTER SIX

Ace stood in the middle of the living room of the presidential suite as Arbella walked in wearing a white see through silk gown. "Hey, bae," he said, eyes rolling over her body. "You look...beautiful. To think, you're all mine."

"Thank you," she said in a hushed tone. "What do you want to talk about? I really wanted to take a nap."

KNOCK. KNOCK.

Ace walked to the door and opened it wide. On the outside four guards covered his room. The waiter in a crisp white uniform glided in, skillfully maneuvering a magnificent cart.

Upon it, a feast fit for a billionaire awaited. The centerpiece was a succulent roasted prime rib, perfectly cooked to a mouthwatering medium-rare, its glistening exterior hinting at the tender meat within. Next to it, trays of steamed lobster tails, their shells a vibrant red. A tower of golden crab legs extended towards the ceiling, their delicate meat waiting to be savored. Along with it a platter of grilled vegetables, bowls of fluffy mashed potatoes, drizzled with melted butter and sprinkled with chives, sat alongside, promising creamy indulgence.

In that moment, the room was transformed into a realm of culinary delight, and Arbella could give a fuck less about any of that shit.

"What am I going to do with all of this food?"

"I ordered your favorites," Ace boasted sitting at the table. "As a matter of fact, I ordered so much I'm not sure what you want."

"None of it."

He glared. "So you're being ungrateful?"

"You asked me what I wanted and I said nothing. How is that ungrateful?"

When the waiter left he sat down at the end of the table. "Sit."

She didn't move.

"Please, baby."

Slowly Arbella walked over to the end of the table and flopped down. Her palms flat. "Thank you."

"Why you sitting like that?"

"What you mean?"

"Stiff."

"I thought you liked mannequins. Women who are better seen and not heard. Women who do what you want without having any real input. Women you can lie to and make feel stupid."

He grabbed a napkin off the table, sat back and dragged a hand down his face. "Stop, sweetheart. You're ruining the moment. We did well today. And that's a win for all of us. Even if you can't see it right now."

"You said you would always love me and yet...yet that's not what I'm getting, Cabello."

"Don't call me that!" He pointed at her.

"But that's the name that you said to call you when you returned from Mexico. The name you were given when your father abandoned you and left you for dead. The name–."

"Not here...that's how I know you don't get it because here I am Banks!"

"You really forgot who you are." She said with disgust. "I thought it was a game, but now I see you really have forgotten."

"Fuck are you talking about? I'm setting up a life for us. The life that if I'm gonna be honest is mine anyway."

"You think being Banks' son entitles you to his money?" She leaned forward. "And to his wife?"

Ace squinted. "I don't know why you so worried about that shit. I told you it was business. *She* is just business."

"She kissed you in that meeting and you kissed her back. And so that makes you a liar because you promised you would never hurt me. But you did that shit in my face."

Ace stood up and stormed toward her. His gray processed hair shining under the soft light as if it were silver. Raising a hand, he smacked her out of her seat. When she tried to get up, he grabbed her by the top of her gown and struck her again.

She smiled, her teeth-tinged red. "See...you are a liar. A shiny one but a liar all the same."

He glared.

"You hit me again. And that will be the last time." She wiggled from up under his grasp and stormed out.

Slowly, the room opposite theirs in the suite opened and Faye exited.

Walking up to him she got on her knees where he remained. "You've outgrown her. The next level requires a bitch like me. And we both know it."

CHAPTER SEVEN

It was well past midnight...

Mason sat on the side of a king size bed staring at a wall. Blakeslee sat opposite of him, her gaze on a mirror. Although she wasn't facing him directly from his reflection, she could see him clearly.

"Can you tell me about your first love?" She didn't know what she was asking but he had chosen to ignore her from the moment they were placed inside the room, and she figured this would be the best way to at least break the silence.

"I remember like it was yesterday."

"Well, tell me about it."

"I knew I would love her for the rest of my life the moment I laid eyes on her. She was the only one who wanted something better. And bigger than what the city offered."

She shifted her body to face him, but he had yet to look at her directly.

"I was young, but I'm the one person that can actually say I experienced love at first sight. And I kept that love in my heart."

"Even now?"

"Especially now." He turned to look at her. "What have you done, Blakeslee? What have you fucking done?"

"I don't know what you–"

"What are you trying to do?! Don't play games with me and find your neck under my fingertips!"

"Nothing! I'm a victim just like you. You...you saw I was in the room with you. And the rest of the family. And the next thing I know I'm being taken out and put in here with you alone. And you hate me for it!"

"You trying to destroy over 40 years of friendship!"

Tears began to fall from her eyes although she hadn't expected it. Blakeslee was very clear about what she wanted. From the moment she saw Mason look at her a bit longer across the room, she knew she had to have him. Because she felt in her heart that she could provide him with the love that he truly deserved.

And he would do the same for her.

Of course it wasn't traditional.

After all, he watched her grow up from a little girl to a woman. But in her mind, she didn't see a problem with such things. In her mind it meant

66　　By T. STYLES

that he helped raise her so that she could be with him. In Roman times young girls were raised for kings until they were the right age.

Couldn't the same be said for now?

Couldn't she be his queen?

"Why you hate me so much? It's obvious your body and soul wants to be with me. Why can't you just allow me to take care of you?"

"You don't know the first thing about caring for a man!"

She stood up. "Then teach me! Show me how to treat you! While you're busy hating me has it ever occurred to you that maybe the thing you prayed for exists in me?! And that if you really want the love you always dreamed about then you have to lose everything to get it! You have to lose who you were! You have to lose your memories! You have to lose my father!"

Mason jumped up and walked around the edge of the bed. He slapped her with the back of his hand on her right cheek and did the same on the left. "I will not let you take him from me!"

She touched both sides of her burning face. "This...this is why you will never get the love you deserve! You don't want to earn it! You want it to be given to you by a person who never will see you like you see him!"

"Stay away from me! Even in this bedroom I don't want you anywhere near me! Don't make me kill you and beg for forgiveness later."

"I won't stop going after what I want," she whispered. "You will be mine."

"Then your days are numbered."

Later that night they both slept.

This wasn't the kind of sleep you got when your heart was at ease. This was a painful sleep. So painful that even in his slumber Mason was rock hard. It's often said that love and hate live in the same neighborhood. But Mason didn't feel that way. He felt lust and hate lived in the same neighborhood. And more than anything both vibrated in his body and his mind.

When she thought he was calm, Blakeslee took a deep breath and eased on top of him. He laid flat on his back like a piece of paper. Damp under the rain. His eyes remained shut.

You up, nigga. She thought to herself. *If you want to fake sleep, have at it.*

Urgently she dug into his boxers and took him and placed him easily into her body. He tried to *fake fight,* but she knew the code.

68

How did she have the code?

It didn't matter. He was inside of her. Moving. Moaning. And he hated that such a young thing looked at him with such power. He hated that she wanted him so much that she was prepared to be ousted from her family.

Because he wasn't.

Mason thought about many things at that moment as he swam inside the wetness of her pussy. He wondered if this ever came out who would Banks choose. Because despite her being Banks' daughter he wasn't sure that she would prevail.

And would it matter?

The pain he would feel if it ever came out was too great for Mason to think about in detail. He would rather kill her and be done with it than to let this shit get out.

Fuck it!

Now they were fucking so he would allow himself relief.

Two more pumps and he exploded in her body, immediately hating himself for it. Tossing her away like a damp rag he leaned to the side and closed his eyes after the hate fuck.

The guilt knocked him right out.

But the next morning when Blakeslee opened her eyes, she had a smile on her face. Until she saw him. Staring at her. He was seated on a chair literally glaring at her with rage in his eyes.

"You are going to tell me what you know about Ace. And you are going to tell me now. Or you will not survive this night."

By T. STYLES

CHAPTER EIGHT

Walid, Dominik, Yazo, and Marco stepped into an elite and secret brothel that masqueraded as a club in Orange Walk. A town known to have the best Belize had to offer. They were looking for one-person and one person only.

Ace Wales.

Still, their senses were immediately engulfed by the electrifying atmosphere. And if you weren't serious you could get caught up. The space was a vibrant symphony of lights, pulsating beats, and a kaleidoscope of colors that made them feel like stars.

Especially Dominik and his friends.

After all, Walid reached deep to make sure they "looked the part" realizing that if they were spotted as "spies" or "cops", that they would be thrown out onto the Belizean streets.

As they hung in the background, they couldn't help but observe all the beautiful women. It wasn't a secret. The country bred some of the baddest women known to man.

Walid and Dominik were focused and looking for the man of the hour, but their friends were in a weird trance.

"Stay focused," Dominik told Yazo. "You know what we doing here."

As they made their way further into the brothel, the thumping bass reverberated through their bodies, infusing them with an undeniable energy. The air was alive with the fusion of urban beats and the intoxicating rhythms of Belize.

The DJs skillfully blended hip-hop, R&B, and trap with the infectious melodies of Punta rock, Kriol, and Brukdown, creating a unique sonic experience that transcended boundaries.

This was for big money niggas.

And Walid and his companions fit in easily.

Their sleek suits, tailored to perfection, showcased their individual styles, and exuded an air of confidence. All of it was on Walid's dime because the last thing he needed was them being thrown out before they could do the work. The club was a playground for fashion-forward men wanting to get their dicks wet and forget their troubles. So they had to look like money.

But they had a purpose.

As Dominik's friends stayed in the heart of the brothel, Walid and Dominik made their way to the bar. A pretty bartender greeted them with a knowing smile. "What you feeling?" She said, her lips glossy pink.

"Give me what you do best," Walid winked, trying to act like the others.

Dominik nodded. "The same."

With that, they turned their backs to her and leaned against the bar...searching...looking...for Ace.

"He's not gonna be here," Dominik announced.

"You can't be sure."

"This is too open. And you said he wanted to be in the trenches. This ain't the fucking trenches. You gotta pay top dollar to be with these ladies."

"True, but it's also not easy to get in and my brother loves privacy. I feel like he'll show up. Plus at this point he's bound to piss Arbella off anyway."

"Did you even ask the rest of your people where he may be?"

"I have a feeling everybody who could raise an alarm are with him. I been calling them all and there are no answers. So he can be here and nobody would think it's weird because no alarms have been sounded."

"So just to be clear, the police are out of the question huh?" Dominik said.

Walid looked at him harshly. "What do you think?"

The bartender handed them their drinks in sleek glassware. Walid chose not to partake but let the rocks clink against the sides to look the part. Dominik on some drunk shit drank the entire glass and asked for more.

Ten minutes later Yazo walked up to them and said, "They know him, but nobody has seen him in years. Used to come with fake IDs because he was under aged. But now he–"

"Hold up, you asked somebody about him?" Walid questioned. "Directly?"

"Yes, figured it was why we were here because–"

"You just put a fucking target on our backs!" Walid put the glass down on the bar, almost sliding it off the top. "Let's get the fuck out of here. Now."

Just as he said that five men in suits moved toward their direction. He could tell by the humps on their hips that they had weapons.

"Let's bounce!" Dominik told his friends as they headed toward the door.

The moment the suits followed them outside, they paused when they saw Dominik's uncivilized goons waiting.

"You don't want bloodshed in front of your establishment," Walid warned. "Go back and enjoy your night. And the ladies."

The head suit in charge said, "Don't come back here again."

Walid nodded and walked away, with rage in his heart.

"I'm sorry, Walid," Yazo said, trotting up to his side.

"Fuck that shit, you owe me one."

Unsuccessful, they hopped in vans and rode off into the night.

Walid sat on the edge of the bed and Aliyah entered. They had an understanding before returning to Belize that she was not his woman. And yet he needed no one else more than her.

"How are you?" She touched his back and then returned her hand to her own lap.

"Existing."

She sat next to him and placed a hand on his leg. He stared at her and she moved it away. "Sorry..."

"I know." He nodded and placed a strand of her hair behind her ear. "I just don't want you thinking anything is different between us. We are not together. I will always take care of you but that's it."

She nodded. "Walid, I'm yours. I said it before and I'll say it again. But I will wait for you to realize it. I will wait for you to change your mind. But you will. I swear."

He sighed.

"I do have to know something, baby."

"What?"

"If you had found Ace tonight would you be willing to go the distance? Would you be willing to–"

"What?" He jumped up. "Are you asking...are you asking me if I would be willing to kill my brother?"

"Walid, I just wanna know if you thought things through. That's it. To the end. Because shit is getting serious."

"That won't fucking happen! I'm gonna find him and talk some sense into him. And don't ever step to me like that again!" He stormed out.

CHAPTER NINE

and talk some sense into him. And don't ever

From Mason and Blakeslee's hotel room, the panorama unveiled a stormy scene in Belize.

Dark clouds hung low in the sky, obscuring the fuck out of the brilliant rays of the sun. Thunder rumbled, accompanied by streaks of neon lightning that smacked across the horizon, illuminating the land below. Rain cascaded down in torrents, while the winds whipped through the palm trees, bending them to their will.

And all Mason could think about was throwing the bitch known as Blakeslee down to her death, hoping it would wash away his betrayal at the same time.

The fact that she has successfully made him her sex slave, using his body the way she desired with a flick of her nails pissed him off. To make matters worse he couldn't resist.

He tried.

God knows he tried.

But this woman reminded him of his true love, and he hated that after so many years he had yet to outgrow the bullshit. A weak crush. Banks would never, ever be his in full.

Right?

With tears strolling down her red puffy face, Blakeslee sniffled. "I promise, I don't know anything about what my brother has planned. I...I don't know why he put you in this room. I don't know why he—."

"You think just because you control my body that you control my mind too?"

"No...I—."

"You will not ruin me! You will not destroy what I've built with Banks. Do you understand?"

She shrugged and cried harder. "And I'm not trying to. I just wanted to spend time with you, so I told him to move us. I didn't know it would make you so mad you'd–."

"So it's true?" He glared.

She fucked up.

She slipped up.

Suddenly the tears went away and she smiled.

"So you did have something to do with this shit? You just said you told him to move us. Now I want to know what you told my son to get him to put us in this place together."

She stood up and walked across the other side of the room. Like a moth she laid flat on the wall. "Nigga, please."

He glared. "What you just say?"

"What's better in lock up than unlimited pussy? You know you wanted to be held up in this bitch the same way I wanted you to be. And the sooner you realize that the happier you will be."

"We will never live *happily ever after*."

"Then we will be *toxically ever after*. Your choice."

"What you know about Ace's plans?"

She peeled herself off the wall and slithered up to him slowly. "I know my brother loves me. And I know he will do what I desire. And I know you better start realizing that I could ruin your life. Is that what you—."

She couldn't have known!

He moved too fast. And before she realized it his hands were around her throat, squeezing the arrogance from her pipes. The plan was simple. He would kill her and beg Banks for forgiveness later.

CLICK.

The door opened, and in rolled a cart filled with food.

By T. STYLES

Quickly he jumped off her and she pulled to her side, coughing the life back into her body.

One man, covered by Big Greasy, entered. "What's wrong with her?" Big Greasy asked.

"I don't know why you doing it, but I know you starving my folks in the other room." He ignored the hell out of him and her hacks on the floor. "And I'm telling you that whatever my son has planned won't work."

"What did you do to her?" Big Greasy asked, looking at Blakeslee.

"I'm...I'm fine," she managed to say. "Please don't tell my brother."

"I don't give a fuck if you tell him or not!" Mason interrupted. "I want you to know that this plan won't end well."

Big Greasy cleared his throat. "You don't know what—."

"Feed my people," Mason said. "Give small gestures. That's all I'm asking for now. Take care of mine with small shit and when things go the other way, and they *will* go the other way, you won't be in the mix."

Big Greasy looked down at Blakeslee who was still having a hard time.

"Fuck her...she good." Mason said. "She done already told you. Do you understand me? Feed my family."

He looked down at her once more, and both men walked out the room.

By T. STYLES

CHAPTER TEN

The room was cloaked in darkness, the only flow emanating from the occasional flicker of lightning that cut through the stormy night was present.

Banks, Spacey, Minnesota, and Joey huddled together, their stomachs growling in hunger. Rain battered against the large windows, blurring the view of the world beyond.

Why was Ace doing this shit?

What was his plan?

How could he starve his own?

Even if he had gripes, did it warrant such torture?

As the thunder roared, the door creaked open, revealing the silhouette of Big Greasy. He stepped into the room, his presence commanding yet serious. For a moment he just looked at their huddled masses. He seemed nervous and jittery.

"Nigga, if you want memories, take a picture and get the fuck out!" Spacey yelled, holding his gut.

"Can you bring it down one notch?" Joey asked his brother. "Please."

"Leave me alone," Spacey responded.

They saw that in Big Greasy's hands, he carried a tray laden with food, a feast that promised slight relief from their gnawing hunger.

Was this for them all, or just Banks?

The Wales clan sat up in attention as they all scanned the tray for what could be eaten now and what would be saved for later. The aroma of warm, savory dishes filled the air, permeating the room and momentarily distracting them from the storm outside.

With relief, Banks, Spacey, Minnesota, and Joey's eyes fixated on the spread before them. The tray held steaming bowls of hearty soup, thick with chunks of vegetables and succulent pieces of meat.

Next to it, plates were piled high with golden-brown fried chicken, crispy on the outside and tender on the inside. The scent of freshly baked bread wafted from a basket, inviting them to tear off a piece and savor its warm embrace.

"Who is this for?" Banks asked cautiously. "Because I'm not gonna keep starving my kids out."

"This a gift," Big Greasy said.

The Wales clan went at it before he could change his mind.

All but Banks.

He didn't eat one morsel.

As they devoured the meal, gratitude filled their hearts. The storm may have raged outside, but within the confines of that room, they found temporary comfort from their captivity and the shared bond that held them together.

Big Greasy exited the room.

"Either this is the best food I ever had in my life or..."

"Is that why your dick hard?" Joey frowned.

Spacey looked down. Sure nuff it was rock hard. "Fuck is you looking for anyway, nigga?"

"I ain't looking! It's too close to the bread for my taste!"

"Both of y'all niggas talking too much," Minnesota said. "If you not saying anything worth hearing, can you at least be quiet while we eat?"

And so they tried.

"You think Ace had a change of heart?" Joey asked, tearing into a chicken wing.

"Nah...this was Mason." Banks smiled, looking out the window.

Spacey grinned. "Feels like him for sure."

In the dimly lit room, shadows danced along the walls as the storm continued to rage outside.

Thunder boomed in the distance, its rumbling echoing through the air like an omen of what was about to unfold. The flickering light from the television dispersed an eerie glow on Arbella's tense figure, her hands trembling as she packed her belongings as quickly as possible.

And then she paused. Her silk garment in her hand. Because Ace, consumed by anger, entered the room.

"You leaving me?" His eyes were red having found out earlier from one of his men what she was preparing to do. "After all I did to find you, you leaving me?"

"Does it matter?"

"Don't play with me, Arbella!" He pointed at the floor. "I have never and will never love a thing as much as you. Don't make me break you apart to prove I can't be without you."

By T. STYLES

She tossed the silk gown in her luggage; angry she was going to take it anyway. She should have left and ordered new things where she landed. But part of her soul was connected to luxurious shit, and so she'd been caught.

"You going too far, Ace. And I can't take it anymore."

The storm seemed to intensify, mirroring the chaos that threatened their relationship. "What is too far?" He yelled; hands clutched in violent knots at his sides. "Everything? Because even everything is not enough for me. For us!"

"You...you are taking all of his money and--."

"You knew my plan!"

"Of course I did! But I didn't realize your plan included her. I didn't realize your plan included...being with her."

"It's just to keep the lie alive so I can--."

"Fuck her! So you can fuck her! Tell the truth! I heard you and her laughing over breakfast. I saw you leaning closer when she gave you her opinions. She is trying to replace me and you're going to let her! So I decided to get out of your way."

Ace was unraveling this much was true. And so he moved slowly toward her. "I promise you that the moment I have what's mine..." he grabbed her hand. "...what's ours, I will let her go."

She stood up, feeling something else coming on. "So you admit, that for now, she is yours." She snatched away.

"You know what I mean."

"It's over, Ace."

He dropped to his knees and wrapped his arms around her waist. "Don't leave me. Don't let me go." He squeezed tightly. "Please, I'm begging you. I'm begging you, baby."

He was a monster, and yet when it came to her, he was putty under her fingertips. But she knew him well enough to know that it didn't mean he couldn't snap seconds later.

Still, she looked down at him. "I'm sorry, I can't do that."

He squeezed her harder. This time so hard he could break her in half. Slowly he rose and looked into her eyes. "Did you think you had a real choice?"

"Ace, what does that–."

"Banks! You may not like it but while we're here you will call me Banks. I've said that before."

"I will not."

He nodded. "Then you bring this on yourself." He walked toward the door. Opening it wide Paulo entered. "Lock her away. Take everything from her but what she has under this dress." He snatched it off. "Maybe then she'll come to her fucking senses."

Paulo smiled as he pulled her away, kicking and screaming.

CHAPTER ELEVEN

The rain continued to pour relentlessly, transforming the streets of Belize into a blurred canvas of wet pavements and dark shadows.

Where was this nigga?

Walid, his determination unyielding, pressed on through the storm in a car that wasn't fit for driving. So he parked on the side of an unknown road to get better views.

This wasn't an unplanned route. He went to the places he'd known his brother to frequent from the past. And as he pushed forward, his body buckled against the fierce gusts of wind.

Still, he scanned the dark and wet streets, searching for any sign, any trace of his elusive twin brother, whose path of deception had led him astray. Led the entire family astray if he was being honest. It was hard looking for your own face as you tried to suppress the hate brewing in your heart.

Yet the young Wales King did just that.

As thunder boomed overhead, echoing through the city, Walid's heart pounded in sync with the beat. His mind raced, consumed by thoughts of the evil that Ace had perpetrated against his own people.

Fuck was wrong with the nigga?

Did he hold no code?

How was it possible for them to be of the same blood, while he was so vicious?

Each raindrop that soaked his face was a bitter reminder of the possible sins committed by his twin who felt slighted. Like somebody owed him something. Like somebody owed him happiness. He continued to press forward, but to no avail. He had yet to find his brother.

Streetlights flickered in the storm's turmoil, showcasing glimpses of the faces of passersby, none of whom resembled the twisted reflection of his own image. But Walid, a real nigga, pressed on, driven by an unwavering sense of justice and the need to protect those he loved.

His father.

His pops.

His sisters.

His brothers.

His nephews.

His niece.

Even his own twin.

Surely he could prevent him from doing so much damage there was no way to return.

After a while he decided to change it up. It was time to go to Ace's old stomping grounds. A place he used to pull Ace out of on so many occasions, he didn't understand why he didn't think of it at first.

Walid's footsteps pumped him to the entrance of a densely lit massage parlor in Gales, the soft glow of neon signs casting an ambiance upon the surroundings.

He could hear the moans.

But did they resemble his brother?

He stepped deeper inside, his eyes scanning the peaceful but dirty space adorned with scented sweet candles to hide the smell of rancid sex in the air.

As he approached the front desk, Walid's voice resonated with a sense of authority. He couldn't shake it if he tried. Rich niggas demanded attention. "I'm looking for my brother."

"Who's your brother?"

"I can tell by the look in your eyes you know he looks like me."

She swallowed. "Ohhh."

"Now have you seen him or not? I don't care about him being underage when he was here. I just need to find him."

The receptionist shook her head.

"Yes or no?" Walid pressed harder, leaning closer to her face.

"No, sir. I haven't." She was lying.

"I'm gonna find out anyway."

Undeterred, Walid ventured deeper into the parlor, weaving through the corridors where soft whispers of tranquil music echoed behind moans. He had a gun on his hip but what was he going to do with it? Was he prepared to buck his brother? Aliyah was right to question him about his intent because it wasn't clarified.

Not to him.

Not to anybody.

Did he have what it took to take his own brother out?

Still, each room he entered held the promise of discovery, a glimmer of hope that he might find Ace. But the universe seemed intent on withholding the answers.

Room after room, Walid encountered strangers, their faces devoid of the familiarity he longed for. A few professionals stopped sucking and rubbing but not one bed had what he wanted to find.

Ace Wales.

Again, it was a bust.

Maybe he wasn't fit to save his people after all.

CHAPTER TWELVE

Ace sat in the scantily lit living room of the opulent presidential suite, his gray silk hair glimmering in the soft glow of the ambient lighting. Beside him rested a glass of amber liquid, the golden hues of whiskey illuminated a warm glow against the polished surface.

Like father, like son.

Because if Banks and Mason enjoyed anything, it was a glass of whiskey.

As Faye entered the room, her beauty was undeniable. Her brown skin, kissed by the sun, emitted a natural radiance that required zero makeup.

Her real black hair flowed down her back, sleek and lustrous like a recently paved road and with each step closer, she exuded a quiet confidence, her poise commanding attention and admiration from him immediately.

"Banks, are you okay?"

He chuckled. "Always in character huh?"

"Shouldn't it be that way?" She smiled. "I mean, didn't you have to put her in her place for not knowing the rules?"

"Be easy with me, I'm fragile."

"You're strong."

As Ace's fingers traced the rim of the whiskey glass, he found himself captivated by the possibilities that lay before him. "You're doing this too well. For me."

"Would you like me to stop?"

"What I would like is for you to give some of your strength to Arbella." The liquid swirled within the glass as he picked it up, mirroring the swirling emotions within his mind.

"Why would I do that?" She shrugged and rolled her eyes.

"Because I'm asking. I want you to get her to understand that all of this will benefit her in the long run."

"And you believe I can do this? For another woman." She laughed. "You forget who you are. You're either the boss, or you're not. You can't have it both ways."

"Be easy with what you say to me."

"You want realness."

"I do. As long as it doesn't border the line of disrespect."

She smiled. Beauty was never Faye's shortcoming and it held Ace's gaze captive even as she pushed her limits. "You never wanted me. Even when I helped you tap Banks' accounts in the beginning it was like...you took from me and when you were done you cut me off. So when Banks reached out, I went with him, hoping it would connect me to you."

"Did it work?"

"I don't know." She shrugged. "After all, I'm here. With you. Right now. Maybe it just took a while."

"I love Arbella."

She moved closer. "And I'm not saying you don't."

"Because you hoping and wishing things will be different but it will never be, Faye. What I need you for is what I'm clear on. The accounts. The lie."

"And yet you would have me suck your dick?" She frowned, pointing at the floor.

"You dropped to your knees on your own."

"And I will do it again."

He shook his head and drank half of the glass. "You entertain me. But as with all entertainment, it ends."

She shook her head.

"I need you for one purpose, Faye."

"You need me for more."

"Nah. I don't."

"You are still trying to be Banks as Ace. And that's not how it works. Wolves and animals higher on the food chain don't worry about the sheep eating. So if Arbella doesn't fall in line, you make the bitch do it, or you get another one. And who better in line than me?"

CHAPTER THIRTEEN

Minnesota was in the bathroom sitting on the floor by the toilet. Her stomach was churning, and she was afraid something deeper was going on. Like illness. Or poison. When the door opened, Spacey entered.

"I heard you out there," he walked deeper inside and closed the door.

"You shouldn't be here." She wiped her mouth with the back of her fist.

"What's wrong with you?" He sat next to her and placed a hand on her knee.

"I don't know."

"Stress?"

"I don't know, Spacey. I really don't."

He sighed. "None of us know what we're feeling for that matter."

Silence kept them for a few more moments. "Do you know...what Ace is doing? I don't get it. I--."

"I don't want to talk about him, Minnesota. I want to talk about you. And if we were to die today, if you have any regrets."

She leaned her head on his shoulder. "Spacey, don't do this to me. I haven't the strength."

"I'm serious. Do you have any regrets about anything? About us."

"Why do you always put me in this position because--."

"I'm not going to touch you. I don't want anything from you. I'm being honest. I really just want to know if you have any regrets about the time we spent at great-grandmother's. Because I always felt like, like I pushed you into something you weren't feeling. Like it was my fault."

"I have no regrets. Being with you at that moment saved my life."

He took a deep breath, and the back of his head touched the wall. "Thank you."

She frowned. "For what?"

"Because I felt like that attic tore us apart and--."

Suddenly, the door flew open and Banks entered. "Fuck is going on in here?"

Spacey jumped up and he helped Minnesota to her feet. "Nothing...I, pops. I was just--."

"I thought I made it clear that whatever weird shit went on between y'all was done!"

"Dad, it's not like that," Minnesota said. "I was feeling bad and he came in here to make sure I was okay."

"Well the door shouldn't be fucking closed!"

Joey walked behind Banks. "What's happening?" He asked. "Y'all making a lot of noise!"

"I caught these two in the bathroom."

"You gotta be fucking kidding me," Joey said. "Why you still pushing up on your sister, nigga?! The shit was wicked at first now you finna go straight to hell!"

"I keep trying to tell y'all it wasn't like that! And I'm sick of feeling like it's a problem with me being there for my sister when we were all we had. And I'm not gonna be scared to talk to her without having a chaperone either. It's fucking simple! We gotta bond."

"Spacey and I understand each other like nobody else. And this dark time, whatever it is, reminds us of that." Minnesota said. "And I'm asking that you don't make it more than it is because you can't handle our relationship. Both of you."

"Food!" A voice called out from the living room. It was Big Greasy.

And once again a cart was wheeled inside but this time it was filled with all crackers and water. The other tray, Banks' tray, had tuna and cheese crackers.

Banks looked at it and then his family.

Almost everyone he loved was in that room.

Almost.

"That's all I could bring. They are watching me now."

"This is your last chance," Banks said to Big Greasy. "Your last chance to save yourself."

"I don't know what you--."

"If my family dies because of whatever deal you have with my son...if they die because you starve them, I will have you tortured like they are being tortured now. So I'm going to say it again. And I want you to know what I'm saying is true. Let us go."

"I don't have the authority to. I'm just--."

"No excuses. I want a yes or no."

"Don't be dumb, man." Spacey interjected. "My stupid ass brother gonna get all y'all niggas killed and you gonna be the first one. If you don't--."

Joey walked up to his brother and dropped him. With a fist to the face.

Spacey passed out.

By T. STYLES

"Fuck you do that for!" Minnesota yelled, rushing to Spacey's side.

"He can take a punch," Joey said. "He'll be alright. But he's the reason Ace ain't listen to Mason last time. And I wasn't about to let it happen again with this man."

Banks dragged a hand down his face, checked Spacey's pulse and rose. Walking over to Big Greasy he asked, "What is your answer?"

Big Greasy looked around. In what felt like forever he said, "I worked for you at the parties you used to throw on your island. You don't remember me, but you were always so kind. So I'm going to help."

Joey was frozen in disbelief. "Wait...what did he just say?"

"Okay." Big Greasy said.

"Okay what?" Joey pressed.

"Okay I will help get you out of here."

Minnesota and Joey stared at him with wide eyes.

"When?" Banks continued.

"I'll do it today. But I need assurances that my family will not just be okay. But well off. College. A new home. All of it!"

"You got it. That's my word." Banks said, extending his hand.

Big Greasy shook his hand. "I'll be back later to help you all escape. I just have to make sure Paulo's not on my tail when I do. Wish me luck."

By T. STYLES

CHAPTER FOURTEEN

Blakeslee and Mason were at their ends.

Yesterday he told her not to utter a word and she said, "I'm tired of trying to get through to you, Mason. If you really want my silence, that's exactly what you'll have. I won't say anything to you again."

And now, he realized silence made him uncomfortable.

It wasn't that he didn't like what quiet brought. The fact that you could hear yourself think without having to entertain. But now he was realizing that silence when you were in the room with an enemy, that you were also sexually attracted to, was difficult.

He needed to hear her talk, even though he hated her so much. "What do you want from me?" He asked.

Silence.

"I mean you put me in this room with you, what do you want?"

Silence.

"So you're gonna sit over there and not speak, Blakeslee?"

Silence.

"Are you fucking serious?"

Silence.

He took a deep breath and sat next to her on the edge of the bed. "Okay...let's talk. For real."

She looked over at him with that cute fucking face he despised.

"I'm sorry for laying hands on you, Blakeslee. But this shit got my pressure up. And I can't believe this is happening to us again."

She smiled. "So you aren't usually this mean to people?"

"This shit just got me messed up. And I need to know what's going on with us. With you."

"Don't worry, Mason. Everything will be okay. You're one of my favorite people so--."

He stood up. "Blakeslee, you say you want to be with me right?"

Her eyes widened. "More than anything in this world."

"Okay, if you want to be with me I need you to tell me what if anything Ace has told you." He looked down at her. "I'm serious."

"He isn't telling me the exact details. He's just--."

"Don't fucking lie to me!" He yelled. "Please!"

She sighed. "He's going to get access to father's accounts. All of them. One by one."

Mason took a deep breath. He had always hoped the children he shared biologically with Banks would be better human beings and he realized it was anything but. "And what else?"

"I'll be guessing at this point but—."

"What fucking else?"

Suddenly the door opened, and Paulo entered. Walking up to Blakeslee he grabbed her by the arm and Mason's heart dropped. "Where you taking her?" He yelled.

"Where she going?!"

He yanked her away, leaving him alone.

Aliyah was on the bed crying when Walid walked inside.

He sat on the edge of the bed and looked down

at her as she continued to weep. "You know I can't do this right now. I don't have the energy. And if you wanna be here you gotta recognize that shit."

She sniffled. "I know."

"So why you doing this to me?"

"I'm not trying to be sad, Walid. I really am not. I just...I guess I just miss our son that's all. And not being able to see him is driving me crazy."

"You know I need him protected. And the last thing I need is someone following you and finding out where he is."

"I know. But what I don't understand is why you wanted me with you instead of with him. It's not like you give me any attention. We barely talk outside of coming up with plans to find Ace which aren't working."

"I want you here because..."

Did he still love her? "Because what?"

"I can't do this right now." He stood up and walked toward the door. Before leaving, he reached in his pocket and removed a phone. After a few clicks he handed it to her.

"What's this?"

"Look at it, Aliyah."

She stared down at the screen and saw Baltimore happily playing in the room from a video camera that was monitoring 24 hours. He had toys, he had games and he had people around him who appeared to make him laugh.

She placed a hand over her mouth and smiled. "Why you didn't tell me you had this?"

"I just put it in yesterday. For you. So it'll make you happy. I just forgot that's all. I'm sorry." He walked out.

She laid on the bed and smiled. As she watched it one thing came to mind, "He still loves me. He still fucking loves me."

CHAPTER FIFTEEN

Arbella lay alone in the room which was meant to be her prison. The space was adorned with lavish furnishings that would take the breath away of someone who knew nothing of luxury. But to Arbella it was an ironic contrast to the sense of captivity that lingered in the air.

The man she met when she was opening her business back in Maryland, who later saved her life and swept her off her feet, was now trying to take her freedom. This was hurtful and devastating because they were supposed to cause havoc together.

The Clyde to her Bonnie, the situation turned into something darker.

She was still thinking about her next steps when Ace entered, closing the door behind him. "Walid is hunting me."

She looked at him and sat up straight, her back against the headboard.

"And I don't know how to handle it." He sat on the opposite side of the bed. "I don't want to hurt my brother, but I will if he gets in my way."

"What do you want with me, Ace?" She wiped her hair out of her face. "It's obvious you don't want a partner. And that you want a slave. I mean look at how you're treating me."

"You mean by giving you the best food, putting you in the best conditions and--."

"You got me in a cotton t-shirt and shorts." She threw back the covers. "Is this what you consider a good life? Because it's not what I envisioned. It's not what we had planned."

"I'll give you better clothes if–,"

"That's not the fucking point! Why you doing this?!"

"Because I don't want you to leave me!" He reached across the bed for her hand, but she pulled back. This angered him but he kept it together. "And I won't have you leave me. And I know you know that."

"I'm not happy, Ace. Just so you know, the moment I can leave I will. You've left me no choice."

His nostrils flared. "Then if you can't play the part, just shut the fuck up and listen!" He yelled, rubbing his temples. "Just...just shut up and fucking listen! I got the entire world coming down on me and I need someone in my corner. Just, just be in my corner."

She laughed and this sent him off the edge.

"What the fuck is so funny?" His neck corded with rage.

"You're losing this war and you haven't even started. I mean, did the tech boys even transfer the money on that deal you and Faye tried to lock?"

"Yes. As much as you hate her she does her part. Unlike you."

Low blow.

"And what about Banks?" She tossed her hands up in the air. "Have you told him to his face what you plan to do? Have you muscled up enough courage to tell him what this is all about? Because I know you're scared."

Ace glared. "It's obvious you still don't know how to treat me. So I'll come back when you have a chance to act right. But I must warn you, I've come too far not to have you on my arm. I've come too far not to have the life I planned for us. When I get our new home, you will either be in my bed or in the grave outside of our bedroom window. But we will be together forever." He stopped by the man at the door. "Don't give that bitch shit else to eat until I say so."

He stormed out.

Ace sat slouched on the deck of the hotel, the midday sun casting a golden glow over the sprawling vista of Belize below.

His drunken state blurred the edges of reality, his senses dulled by the whiskey he had consumed. As he stared out into the distance, his eyes wandered, searching for something that might distract him from the guilt he felt in his heart.

His girl hated him.

His family despised him.

And the city told him his twin was coming. Although Ace wasn't roaming the slums or hanging in the rougher parts of town, he still kept a few connections. He was in the know enough to know Walid was serious about finding him. And Ace also knew he was the only one who could get a hold of him if he tried.

Besides, they had the same DNA. They had the same mind. They shared the same womb. Flew out of the same pussy.

So he had to be careful.

"Brother..."

It was then that Blakeslee, switched out on the deck after being snatched out the room she shared with Mason by his men. She looked whorish while wearing a red strappy dress and the moment she saw his face she approached cautiously.

"Ace..." She stood before him with clenched hands. "Is everything okay? I mean, are you well? Why have you summoned me?"

"You asked about Mason, but not your own daughter."

She glared. "You and I both know Sugar belongs to Minnesota."

"What a mother."

She rolled her eyes. "What is this about?"

"You're beautiful," he said in a low voice. "Beautiful women have so much power. And it's unfair."

"Are you angry with me?"

"Should I be?"

"Brother, what's happening? If I wronged you in some way let me know so that I can make it right."

"What's going on with you?" He said plainly. "And don't fucking lie to me, Blakeslee." He was on edge and he knew it. "I need truth from a woman that I love."

"Look, you've been drinking and—."

"What do you want with my fucking father?" He yelled. "And why are you so fucking obsessed with older men?! It's a sickness that's unnatural. It's a sickness that–."

"Maybe I'm looking for a daddy figure. Like you're looking for a mommy figure in Banks, which you'll never find."

This bitch tried it.

"You think I won't hurt you. You think I won't snap your neck, but I will. I swear to God I will."

Blakeslee, her demeanor guarded, hesitated for a moment before meeting his gaze. "I hate when you talk to me this way."

"Then do better and answer the fucking question. What do you want with my father?"

She looked outward.

At the horizon.

The view before them stretched far and wide, a mesh of the city and nature intertwining in a dance. Palm trees reached toward the blue sky, nearby resorts speckled throughout their glass windows reflecting the sunlight, while lush greenery reminded them both of Belize's vibrant beauty.

"I want him. And I gotta have him."

He glared. "You want him? What does that fucking mean?"

"He's your father not mine. And I want a life with him. I want him in all ways possible. And I know you understand."

"Don't push me. In case you haven't realized I'm not the same nigga you grew up with. The innocence I once held was washed away a long time ago."

She shook her head. "You were born a monster so you were never innocent. And don't be angry about it, brother. Because so am I."

"This thing with my father is gross. He watched over you since you were a baby."

Blakeslee, her youthful features tinged with a mixture of defiance and vulnerability, chose her words carefully. "I want that man. I want to be with him. And I think he's the only person who can keep me alive in this family."

"The only person? Who am I?"

"Until you finish whatever you are doing, I'd have to say yes."

He nodded.

116

At least there was the truth.

"If it ever came down to it...if..." he took a sip and a tear rolled down his face. "If it ever came down to it, who would you choose? Me or him."

She moved closer and got on her knees between his legs. The roughness of the concrete scratched her skin, bringing a thin sheet of blood to the surface. "Brother, in a heartbeat I would throw that nigga off the side of the building if it meant saving you."

He put his glass down, bent over and kissed the top of her head.

She stretched her neck up and kissed him on the lips. A passionate kiss, too close for brother and sister.

Paulo rushed onto the balcony. "Banks, something has happened. Come now!"

CHAPTER SIXTEEN

Banks, Joey, Spacey, and Minnesota sat in the unilluminated hotel room, their hunger gnawing at their stomachs.

"I knew he wasn't coming back," Spacey said about Big Greasy, his eye still blackened due to Joey's whop to the face. "I don't know why you trusted it, pops. We out here on our own."

"I know when a man is telling the truth. And he was telling the fucking truth. Something else happened."

"It was probably Spacey's dumb ass," Joey said under his breath.

"Nigga, shut the fuck up."

As the door creaked open, Ace stumbled into the room, pushing a cart adorned with a large pot and a manila folder. On this cart was a beautiful gold pen. Ace's disheveled appearance and the lingering scent of alcohol that clung to him put them all on immediate guard.

But what Banks noticed was that he couldn't look directly at him. Guilt and desperation danced in his bloodshot eyes as he finally faced his father.

"You have always thought you controlled me. Haven't you?"

Banks' jaw twitched.

"And I know I'm of your blood, but you don't own me. You never have or never will."

"Brother, what's going on?" Joey asked calmly. "Whatever you're going through, we can make it right. It's not too late, man. I been talking to pops and I'm telling you it's not too late. Why you doing all this?"

"Ace, please let us go," Minnesota begged. "I wanna go home. I wanna get out of here."

He looked at her and shook his head. "You know you never fucked with me. Ever. And now you fix your lips to say my name?"

"Siblings fight!" She yelled at him. "Why is that so hard to fucking understand? Huh?"

"Son, what do you want from me?"

He looked at Banks. "Sign over all your bank accounts if you want to be free," Ace demanded, his words straight to the point. "Give me all."

"I told you this nigga wanted to be you!" Spacey yelled. "Y'all believe me now?"

"Spacey, stop!" Banks responded, pointing his way. "I don't want you to say anything else tonight!"

"Dad, if you sign over your accounts he will kill us all," Spacey pleaded. "I'm sorry but it's true."

"Sadly, I agree," Joey added.

"So once again it's all about money?" Banks said calmly to Ace.

"Isn't everything about money?"

"No, son. It's not. It doesn't have to be this way. It doesn't have to be like this. And you know it."

"Sign the papers, dad."

"Pops, you can't do it!" Spacey yelled.

"Sign the fucking papers!"

Banks, weary yet resolute, met his son's gaze, his features a mask of frustration. The weight of his decisions and the consequences sat heavily on his shoulders.

He knew that giving into Ace's demands might be their only chance at survival, but the price of his freedom was a bitter pill to swallow. At the same time, what was to stop him from betraying him?

Betraying the entire family once he got what he wanted.

Once he got everything.

"Where is Mason?" Banks asked.

"He's fine."

"What does that mean?"

He smirked. "It's funny that you're asking about my father, but you haven't asked about Blakeslee."

"Because I know she's safe. I know she's in contact with you. I saw her phone."

Joey's eyes widened and he looked at his father. "You mean you knew she had a phone and you ain't let us yank it from her ass?"

"They have this place locked down. The Belizean police are out of their league and some are corrupt. It would do us no use."

Spacey shook his head. "Wow."

Banks refocused on his son. "Ace, it's not too late too--."

"You left me in fucking Mexico, nigga!" He roared. "You took everything from me! I had no clothes! I had no shoes and I had no food! I was fed by a boy who allowed me to eat with his dog because his father wouldn't miss the extra food if he was feeding an animal. Sign the fucking papers!"

"You tried to kill us!" Banks yelled for the first time. "And now you standing in front of me, trying to do it again!"

Spacey laughed.

"What's so funny, nigga?" Ace asked him.

"You know who else was fed by a child when we were locked in an attic? Me and Minnesota. And you know who that child was who saved our lives? Walid. And when he finds us, and he will find us, he gonna kill your punk-bitch ass."

Ace reached behind his waist and grabbed a gun. Yanking Spacey by his collar he put the gun to his head and cocked.

Banks felt faint.

Knees weakened.

So did Minnesota and Joey as they pleaded for Spacey's life.

"Ace, please!" Banks begged with outstretched arms. "Please don't do this shit. I'm begging you."

Ace's eyes were wild and crazy as he aimed the weapon at Spacey, Joey and Banks as they made small movements toward him.

"Please...please don't kill my son," Banks pleaded.

It was the first real emotion he'd shown.

"He's not even your blood." Ace said.

"I watched him grow up to be a man." His palms were in his direction. "I was with him as a baby. I raised him. He *is* my son. And I'm begging you not to take his life."

Tears rolled down his cheek. "You love this nigga more than me. Don't you? You've always loved him more than me!"

The room, a silent witness to their familial strife, became a battleground of conflicting emotions.

"DON'T YOU, FATHER!" He pressed the barrel to his head so hard it was leaving an indentation mark on his skin. "YOU LOVE HIM MORE THAN ME! SAY IT! FUCKING SAY IT!"

"Ace, please don't kill him. I'll sign the papers. I'll give you whatever you want. But not if you take his life."

Ace looked down at Spacey and knocked him out with the butt of the gun. Next he stood up, wiped the tears from his eyes and put the gun in the back of his pants.

"You called war when you tried to get my man to turn against me. His death is on your hands. If you really want a truce, I'll send Paulo back to get the signed papers. The choice is yours."

Which man was he talking about? They wondered.

When he left Banks and Joey put Spacey on the bed while Minnesota sat in the corner crying.

"This nigga been getting his ass whooped all week," Joey said shaking his head as he looked after his brother. "I hope he shut the fuck up now."

Slowly Banks moved to the pot on the cart. When he raised the lid, he saw that inside was Big Greasy's head.

CHAPTER SEVENTEEN

Walid was fucking tripping...

Walid ventured into the crime-ridden heart of Belize like he wasn't worth a billy. Driving a broken-down Honda to "blend in" with the gritty streets pulsed with danger, a testament to the darkness that permeated every corner. With every mile, he felt the weight of the world pressing upon him, the urgent need to save his family fueling his soul.

As he navigated the alleys, shadows danced around him. He tried to look like the locals, but he shined too bright despite having on zero jewelry or designer labels.

Still the air was heavy with tension, the distant sounds of sirens and echoing footsteps serving as a haunting reminder that he wasn't on his island anymore. The flickering streetlights beaconed an eerie glow on everything evil about Belize.

Walid's heart pounded in his chest, as he scanned the faces that passed him by. It was in the midst of this urban chaos that his worst fears materialized.

Suddenly, a group of shadowy figures emerged from the darkness, their intentions nefarious and their hearts filled with malicious intent. But he didn't seem bothered.

He saw something he wanted to investigate from the past.

He parked his car and walked up to an old house where a woman Ace liked to check out lived. Because when they were on the island, Ace preferred the streets, and this hood was his stomping grounds. When he was closer one of the men asked, "Which twin are you?"

Silence.

He was recognized.

"I asked are you a Wales?"

"Nah."

"Take your hood off so we can see your face."

"Nigga, fuck you!"

And so they jumped him.

Their grip like steel vices, as they did their best to drag him into the depths of their underworld where their actions could not be seen. In the moment desperation fueled Walid's fight for survival, his instincts guiding him as he unleashed a flurry of punches and swift movements. It was

126

three on one as he battled against the odds that threatened to take his fucking life.

With sheer determination, while also seeing his son's face in his mind, Walid managed to break free from their clutches. Gasping for breath, bloodied, and bruised, he raced through the dark streets, the sound of pursuit echoing behind him.

Every step brought him closer to safety before he jumped in a car waiting on the curb. "Go!"

"Who are you?" The stranger asked.

He looked behind him at the assailants who were still on his heels. "JUST GO! I'LL GIVE YOU A BUNCH OF MONEY AND IT WILL CHANGE YOUR LIFE!"

The man took off leaving the goons in the rear.

Fifteen minutes later he was at Aliyah's aunt's house. Finally reaching the door, Walid burst through, his chest heaving and sweat dripping down his brow. Aliyah and Dominik, their eyes wide with concern, rushed to his side.

Walid dashed to the back, came out with fifteen stacks, and handed it to Yazo. "Pay the driver."

"I got it!" He ran out to do what was asked.

"I can tell by the look on your face shit didn't go as you planned!" Dominik glared. "I told you not to go anywhere without me and my guys! Why didn't you fucking listen?"

Walid walked past him and flopped on the sofa. "I was trying to blend in."

"Are you fucking crazy. You will never blend—"

Aliyah touched Dominik's arm, calming him down. "Let me talk to him. Please."

Dominik shook his head. "Either you want our help, or you don't, Walid. But it can't be both!" He stormed out.

In the confines of Aliyah's aunt's house, the air hummed quietly as he walked to their room.

Once inside, Aliyah closed the door and leaned against the frame. "Walid, you're not using your head. You aren't being smart, baby."

"I don't get it. I'm doing everything I know to find him. I'm in the streets looking, searching. But there's no sign of him. Nowhere! And my family may be...my family may be–"

"Don't say it." She moved closer. "The problem you have is that you're thinking about old Ace. Ace from when you were kids. But if you're right, that he's trying to be Banks, doesn't that mean he will move like him too?"

CHAPTER EIGHTEEN

The sun flooded its warm rays upon the vibrant world below, illuminating the waters of the pool where people reveled in the joys of life.

From the window of the luxurious hotel, Mason gazed out hating every smiling face he saw. He knew it wasn't right, but so much weighed on his heart in the moment, that he didn't want to see anyone else's happiness.

When Ace first started wilding out, he was the one who told Banks not to kill their son. He was the one who threatened their friendship if Banks ever laid hands on him. Mason was the one who wanted to keep him alive. And to think that his decision of wanting his son to change would be the reason for their demise, fucked with his mind.

And then there was Blakeslee.

Where was she?

Where had they taken her?

And why was she removed so abruptly?

His mind wrestled with conflicting emotions, his love-hate relationship with Blakeslee made the heart heavier. Maybe if they killed her he could be done with her. But how would he really feel about that shit?

And what about Banks.

Could he lose another child, even one he was certain was not his favorite?

Tossing himself on the edge of the bed, he kept his gaze out the window and on the sky. And then the door swung open, and there stood Blakeslee.

She looked clean.

She looked healthy.

But more than it all she was alive.

He rose, his heart skipped a beat as he took in her presence. For the moment he put the dumb shit to the side because he realized he was relieved. Relief so heavy he felt more guilt. "Are you okay?"

She nodded.

"Did they hurt you?"

She shook her head no.

"What...what happened?"

"I thought you didn't care about me."

He glared. "Don't fuck with me."

"I'm okay." Her gaze lowered to the floor and then back into his eyes. "Thank you for asking. And for caring."

Despite the bitch she had come to be, her demeanor softened by the look in his eyes. They stood apart from one another. Just staring.

"Can I move closer to you, Mason?"

He nodded yes.

She eased toward him, took his hand, and sat with him on the edge of the bed. The sides of their legs touched, and the attraction was electric. "They just took me and asked questions."

"About?"

"About you."

"If you want me like I believe you do, you have to be honest with me. You have to tell me what—."

"He's my brother, Mason! I can't tell you everything we discuss. That's not fair."

"And he's my fucking son!" He jumped up and stood in front of her.

"You know...sometimes when you yell you get my pussy wet. And other times when you yell you scare me."

Silence.

"Right now I'm afraid."

He took a deep breath, paced a few and leaned against the wall across from where she sat. "Okay...I'm...I'm sorry."

She nodded. "Like I told you before they removed me my brother...Ace...wants the money."

"Did he say how much? Did he say anything else?"

"He won't tell me about his plans, Mason."

"Why? It's obvious you got some fucking pull."

"He won't tell me his plans because of you."

He shrugged. "I don't get it."

"I told him I wanted you. So he can't trust me the same."

Mason felt dizzy. "Wanted me like what?"

"You know."

"So...so he knows we...he...fucked?"

"Does it matter?"

Mason dragged his hands down his face. "This shit is going to crush Banks. It's going to crush him in ways—."

"Ace won't tell him!"

He glared. "How the fuck do you know?"

"Because while my brother may be mad at him, he wouldn't wanna hurt me."

"You may be right. But that would only be if he had intentions on keeping him alive. And you and I both know he wants him dead."

In Banks' room, everyone but him was asleep. And he was grateful for the privacy.

His children were all adults, but that didn't make shit any easier seeing the hunger pangs that were starting to make their way to their thinning faces. Time passed by and then for some reason Spacey stirred on the floor, opening his eyes fully. Followed by Joey and Minnesota who were asleep on the bed.

Still, they respected the silence as a sense of unease hung heavy in the air. Spacey, Joey, and Minnesota exchanged worried glances, their instincts alert to the growing tension that enveloped their family. Without shit being said they all knew this very well may be the end of the Wales saga.

"What you think he has planned?" Spacey asked, breaking the silence.

"You keep asking the same shit." Joey yelled. "The nigga came in here, bust you in the face and told you what he wanted. How many times you gonna ask the same shit?"

134   **By T. STYLES**

"I have to talk, man. I have to say something because at this point, I'm going crazy. Hearing other voices outside of my own makes me think...makes me feel that at least I'm alive. For now."

"He's going to kill us," Minnesota said plainly. "I mean did you see the look in his eyes? He's gonna kill us, starting with Spacey."

"Hold up, why me?" He threw his hands up in the air.

"Whatever goodbyes we've been wanting to say, we can do them now," she continued.

"No goodbyes," Banks said plainly looking into each of their eyes. "Do you hear me? Not one of you better let go. Not one of you better give up. We've been through this shit before."

"I don't know, pops. This feels different. It--."

"Skull Island?" Banks said, reminding them how they came out on top of that situation.

They nodded.

"The shootout in Baltimore that Arlyndo and Minnesota caused," Spacey added. "We still alive after that one too."

"Somebody always bringing that shit up," she said. "Get over it."

"We been through shit," Banks said firmly. "And we gonna get through whatever this is too. But I just need to..." he walked to the window. "I need to think. I need to think clearly."

The room seemed to shrink, its walls closing in on them as the door swung open, revealing the ominous presence of Paulo.

Paulo, with a hardened gaze, stomped with a purpose that sent shivers down their spines. His henchmen flanked him, letting every Wales-Born know that they wanted all the smoke.

"Where is the pen you were left to sign the papers?" Paulo asked Banks. "Ace said he left them here."

"I don't know."

"WHERE IS THE FUCKING PEN!"

Banks remained as still as a statue. "I just told you I don't know."

Paulo laughed. "You will pay for this, and you will use it to write a letter to your family, before I take your life."

Without another word, Paulo gestured for Spacey, Joey, and Minnesota to follow, his intentions veiled in darkness.

"Where are you taking them!" Banks roared.

"Didn't I tell you that I don't have to answer to you?" Paulo laughed. "Why don't you get it?"

The men laid hands on Minnesota, Joey and Spacey as they dragged them toward the exit. A surge of adrenaline coursed through their veins as the three attempted to break free from the clutches of their captors.

Even Banks considered going hard and knocking at least one out.

But losing his kids would surely bring him to his knees and send him to an early grave.

The three lunged forward, backward and from side to side, but Paulo's men were prepared and stronger. In a swift and coordinated move, they overpowered their resistance, and moved them closer to the door.

Banks walked up to Paulo.

He said nothing.

Just stared.

"Problem?" Paulo asked.

Banks smiled.

"Remember this moment," Banks said clearly.

"But of course," he shrugged as he exited with Spacey, Joey, and Minnesota, their pleas echoing through the hallway.

At some point Minnesota grew tired of trying to save herself. The lack of meals caused her body to lose esteem. Lose its energy.

Was this part of Ace's plan too?

Because it was working.

Before long Joey and Spacey also lost the will as they were ushered down the hall, the weight of their situation pressing upon them with each agonizing push. Their freedom slipping through their fingers like grains of cocaine.

As they were led further into the unknown, Spacey, Joey, and Minnesota exchanged a silent pact, a shared understanding that they would not give up.

They were Baltimore bred.

They may have always been wealthy, but they were also of the streets.

Their resolve burned brighter, fueled by the Wales bonds that forged through their blood.

"Don't give up," Joey mouthed. "Don't give up."

CHAPTER NINETEEN

Ace was on his second bottle of whiskey for the morning.

Since he was beefing with Arbella, he was realizing that what he was trying to do would mean nothing without her.

And then there was his brother. Word had gotten back from Paulo that Walid was somewhere in Belize trying to find him. The thought of his twin brother, Walid, relentlessly searching for him gnawed at his conscience, a constant reminder of the tangled web of deception he had woven.

He didn't even allow himself to think about his brother for too long. Because it was a sore, sore topic. But he missed him. Loved him and didn't want them to be at war despite knowing that Walid would always be loyal to Banks.

He would always be loyal to the Wales'.

And that made him an enemy.

Seeking the love of his woman, he made his way to Arbella's room. Nodding at the guard, the door was opened and he entered. As usual, she was standing by the window, looking outward.

"You look beautiful."

She remained with her back in his direction. And the anger radiated from her in a way he couldn't help but feel. She wanted her freedom.

And if the nigga wasn't with it, she wanted off with his head.

He tried to make her feel like she had a choice to love him.

She didn't.

The room, adorned with a spread of delicious food, stood as a stark contrast to the bully outside her door who would not let her leave. He even sent her a beautiful soft pink silk nightgown that attacked her sexy curves at the moment.

"You aren't eating."

"What do you want?"

"Even though you mad, your voice still recharges me."

"Ace, I want nothing to do with you." She looked at him and his heart broke when he saw the hate in her eyes. Yep, it was real. "But if you're into speaking to walls, do so. Just leave me out of it."

She faced the window again.

"I saw my father the other day."

She looked at him. This was interesting. Especially if the meeting brought about an end to her prison sentence.

"I told him to sign the papers."

"Did he?"

"He said he would." He paused. "But my brother has been looking for me harder now. So I don't know if it will matter. The bankers don't seem to want to put the assets in my name, so everything is on hold."

"Which brother is looking for you? You have many."

"The only one who counts. The only one that's free."

"Walid loves his family."

"And I don't?"

She laughed.

"Fuck is so funny?"

"You love your family? So who are them niggas you got held up in rooms on this floor?"

"I'm talking about you, Arbella. I care about you. And you are my family."

Silence.

"If he finds you, what will you make of him?"

"He's my brother."

"And yet that's not an answer."

"I don't know." He looked down and wished he bought the liquor bottle with him because he needed relief. "I'm confused."

"Where is your other woman, Ace? Why bring these things to me?"

"Don't play."

"Where is she?"

Ace's presence elicited a conflicted response from Arbella, her anger and envy simmering beneath the surface. The realization that Ace had grown closer to Faye, ignited a bitter pang of jealousy within. And she hated that shit. Back in the day if a nigga did her wrong she could ignore him and move on with her life.

But he was her life.

There was nothing left.

"You're mad about what doesn't matter."

She laughed. "The original plan had been for Faye to play a role not to become the role."

"And she's not."

"Oh...is that so? Is she locked up too or is it just me?"

Silence.

"That's what I thought." She sat down, her back in his direction.

142   By T. STYLES

As Ace's eyes fell upon the untouched food, guilt and concern etched across his features, he longed to bridge the growing divide between them. To put shit back in its original form sooner than later.

"You must eat, baby."

"Leave me alone, Ace. Go back to your new wife. Or should I call you Banks?"

"You will love me again." He spoke. "I swear to God."

"I never stopped loving you. That's why this shit hurts so much." She shook her head. "Now get the fuck out of my cell!"

CHAPTER TWENTY

In Banks' room, he was lying in bed although sleep was nowhere near.

He had worked out so many plans in his mind, and the various ways shit could go down all ended badly. And then the air crackled with tension as Domingo, a Belizean man of authority, entered.

"Did you sign the other papers?"

He looked at him. "Where are my children?"

"You mean them grown ass adults who--."

"Where are they?" He rose to his feet.

"Where are the papers, sir? Don't make me get angry and do things to them you can't see within the halls of this hotel."

Banks pointed. "Over by the TV."

He walked toward them, picked them up and presented him with another stack of papers for his signature. "He wants you to sign these too. The sooner you can do it the better."

"I need a pen."

Domingo looked at him. "I'm going to hand you this pen, but you won't lose this like the other one.

And I'm going to stay right here to watch it go down."

Banks laughed once. "Like I told you, I don't have the pen."

"Sign!" He pointed down with a big beefy finger, which also held the pen. "Now."

Banks grasped the pen in his hand, acutely aware of the weight of his actions.

As he carefully scrawled his signature across the document, he remembered who he was. Unlike his best friend he was always able to keep his calm and talk his way out and into anything.

"How much is he paying you?"

"Sir, please sign."

Banks put the pen down. "You will get every document signed you want. And I'm willing to do much more. Right now, I'm asking you to be a man and talk to another one. Show some humanity. Please, sit."

It took a moment, but he complied.

"How much is he paying you?"

"Enough."

"For your soul?"

"This isn't going to cost me my soul. I'm just doing a job. And I'm sure you've done much worse."

"I've done things that would keep you and your children up at night. But every time I was forced to do much worse, I reasoned. I made sure that the decision I would have to make hit only those involved. Whether it was in the streets or in the stock market I'm always careful to make the right moves." He paused. "So, how much?"

"Five thousand dollars."

Banks' heart dropped. "So that's the going rate for a billionaire's life?"

"That's enough to--."

"Do nothing." Banks' voice carried a tone of resolute determination. "That is not enough to change your life."

"Maybe not to you."

"To nobody." He picked up the pen and began to sign again.

"Then how much is it worth?" Domingo said. "A billionaire's life?"

Out of the man's view Banks smiled. "A million."

Domingo's heart pumped as he listened to how Banks declared himself a businessman, asserting his belief that his vast wealth would ultimately grant him the freedom and power he sought in his own country.

146

"You would give me a million?"

"You are a man of the streets. Ask about me. They will tell you I keep my word. That's the Wales Warranty. But if you aid my son Ace, your family will be murdered. So you will lose even more."

"Don't threaten my people."

"Why not? This entire situation is threatening mine."

Domingo, his gaze unwavering, listened to Banks' defiant words. "But what about Marcus?"

Banks squinted. He didn't know the person.

"The one you had killed."

He was referring to Big Greasy, but he never knew his name.

"He was a good man. He chose to help and Paulo ordered the removal of his head."

The weight of the consequences settled upon the room, a chilling reminder that in the games of power and money, there were casualties...always.

"You are right. But Marcus was not smart."

"That's not fair, sir."

"It may not be but it's true. If he were smart, he would be here. He told somebody. Made some wrong moves. And you will not do the same."

"But I have a family."

"I do too, nigga," Banks said through clenched teeth. "I do too. And I'm fighting for mine. What the fuck you think you gonna do for yours with $5,000? I'm prepared, right here, right now to make you a millionaire!" He pointed at the floor. "That's life changing money!"

Banks recognized the harsh reality of war, where choices had consequences and alliances shifted with treacherous ease.

"But you have to pick a side. And you have to do it now, son!"

"Please sign the papers, sir. They are waiting on me."

Banks nodded.

He knew he had him, whether the man realized it or not.

Walid was coming up short on the hunt for his brother.

He needed fresh air.

As he walked the bustling streets of Belize, a few miles away from the slums, the energy of the city enveloped him. With each step, he felt a sense of purpose pulsating through his veins.

And then something happened.

He was recognized but in a gentle way. Strangers approached him with gratitude, expressing their appreciation for his contributions to the rough parts of the city. Their words struck a chord within him, igniting a newfound determination to confront his evil brother.

"You're not like the other one," one woman said.

"You have kind eyes," said another.

Among the grateful individuals, a woman named Maria approached Walid moments later, her eyes brimming with heartfelt appreciation.

"You...you are Walid Wales."

He nodded, not sure at first how to take her. "Yes, ma'am. I am. How could you tell me from my brother?"

She laughed. "You didn't enter homes without asking. You aren't yelling or making yourself seen. You're trying to connect with my country here on the streets. When you could be in a nice cool hotel, living your life. That's how I know."

And then she told him the story of how Banks provided financial means for her mother's life-saving transplant. She went on to talk about the home he put her family in, which she still cherished to the day.

The depth of the impact the Wales family's generosity had made on the lives of others struck him with a renewed sense of purpose.

"Kindness impacts people in ways I can't explain. Always remember that, son. Love comes back and rewards."

"Thank you."

"No, thank your father. I'm praying for him."

Walid wished he could, he missed him so much.

With a surge of inspiration, he hurriedly made his way back to Tia's house where Dominik and his friends awaited.

Aliyah quickly entered the living room where they all were posted up. "Are you okay?" She saw light in his eyes for the first time in a long time.

"Yes...I'm good, baby." He focused on Dominik. "I need you to hit up your friends and tell them I want to speak to them, but it has to be kept on the low."

"It'll be hard but—."

"Maybe but it has to be done." Walid said firmly. "Ask only those who can hold water."

He nodded. "Asking only the loyal, thins out my prospects, but I can do it." Dominik nodded. "Now what exactly am I asking them?"

While speaking to the woman, a realization dawned on Walid — his evil twin would not be found in the slums, but rather in a place of luxury and grandeur.

The ally had said don't come to the resort, but every place he went there was no sign of his family. That's because Ace had to have help from people who worked wherever he had them.

"Like Aliyah was saying, I was thinking of my brother when we were younger. But he always wanted power. He always wanted to be my father. So why would he come back here?"

"I'm still lost," Dominik said.

"He's at a hotel. One of the richest ones in this country."

"Wait, you think he's in a hotel while he got your people out here in the slums?"

"Nah...he has them with him." He paused. "He can't trust that someone will go against him by leaving them here while he is in a hotel. One Wales family member can change a life for the right ransom if a kidnapper gets a hold of one."

"True," Yazo said.

"Hold up, you think he's holding your family hostage at a hotel? Even though you checked quite a few after the lady called. She said specifically *"don't come to a resort"* which meant they aren't there."

"I think the person thought I had been given the name of the resort they were in, but I was checking me and Aliyah into a hotel since our island burned down."

"Brother, there is no way Ace has an entire family held up at no luxury resort or hotel." Dominik laughed. "Because I can't see him doing it out in the open."

"Is that why if you look on the back of every hotel door here you see *'if you're being trafficked call this number'* signs?"

Dominik wasn't smiling anymore.

Walid was right.

"We are looking for hotel workers. This is an inside job. And when we talk to them, we need to find out about weird guests. Who have particular needs. Things like guests don't want their rooms cleaned. Or tell them not to come on this floor. At the end of the day, if he has them held up like that, he blocked off rooms. Maybe even floors. Somebody knows something."

Dominik and Yazo smiled.

Aliyah happily wrapped her hands around Walid's waist and hugged tightly. "I think you're right, Walid. I think you're right!"

He grinned.

CHAPTER TWENTY-ONE

Blakeslee was on top of Mason, looking down into his eyes.

The lights were out as the moon from the open window outlined her frame. It may have been twisted, but as Mason pushed up into her warm body, he told himself that she was the love of his life.

And like she was a weird artificial intelligent version; she played the part.

"Damn, this dick feels so good," she said, biting down into her bottom lip. "I...I love how you move inside of me, Mason."

Pulling her onto his chest, his dick remained tucked as he suckled her right breast. She was wetter than he imagined, and he could leave his eyes open and pretend she was really Banks before he transitioned.

"Why you make me wait so long?" He breathed heavily. "Huh? Why you make me wait so fucking long?" He continued, feeling himself about to explode.

Blakeslee got what was happening.

She was to not be herself.

But to be Banks.

"I'm sorry..." She moaned as she moved up and down, her juices drenching his pulsating dick. "But I'm...I'm here now, baby. I'm here now."

He pumped harder. Stronger and more aggressive.

"Oh my...oh my gawd...Mason I'm about to..."

Hearing her about to reach the point he pushed her off and said, "Suck it. Every drop."

Moving to her knees she opened her mouth and allowed him to grab both sides of her face as he exploded his cream between her lips. Her pink tongue glistened after she swallowed every ounce.

But she continued to suck until every drip had vanished.

When he was done, he laid on his side and she crawled in front of him. They were in the aftermath of their betrayal. Still wet with sweat and sex.

The air between them was thick because they were at a new level.

A dangerous level.

As they caught their breath, Mason's voice broke the silence. "This can only work if you know what I need."

"I do."

"Do you really?"

"Did I not satisfy you just now?"

"That's the youth in your mind. I don't need you to be you, I need you to be the woman I always wanted. There's a difference."

"Then teach me."

He chuckled.

"I'm serious. I don't understand what this thing is you have for my father. He's too mean and old for me to understand."

"Everyone will age." He paused. "Even you."

"I know, and I don't mean it that way. It's just that...I don't get it. Your love for him. But it doesn't mean I won't get it for you. All you have to do is teach me how to act and be."

"You will never have my heart the way you want. You think you will, but I need you to understand. If we make it out of this alive, it will never be how you want it to be." His words-tinged caution.

"That hurts, Mason."

"I gotta deal with the power you have over me. But the moment you forget that you're an avatar, we are done."

His admission hung in the air, a delicate truth that threatened to unravel the fragile bond they

156

had forged. But Blakeslee brushed aside his reservations. With a voice filled with unwavering resolve, she said, "Fuck up my life. I don't even care no more." To her, even a taste of his fabricated affection was preferable to a life devoid of love. A life devoid of him.

"You sound crazy."

"Has it ever occurred to you that my father not wanting you the way you want him is why we're here? Maybe I am his karma."

"That...that may be true but—."

"We can't go back now, Mason. That's all I know. Even before the hotel we made love, in my room. And I'm not willing to let that go."

In the vulnerability of that moment, Mason shared a haunting truth. "If he ever finds out he will kill us."

"Then we will die. Together."

The reality of their situation hung heavy in the room, clouding their new connection. Unfazed by the threat, Blakeslee said, "I know I'm a whore to my family. But you never saw me that way. So I will always, always go where you want. Be who you want and do what you want." She said with fierce loyalty.

"But what about Ace?"

Silence.

"Blakeslee, you're willing to fight your father, my friend, but what of Ace? If it came down to it, who will you choose?"

"He asked me that when I saw him. Who would I choose."

"What was your answer?"

"I said him."

Her honesty put a smile on his face because at least she told the truth.

"I lied. I choose you. I choose us."

Her unwavering devotion pierced through the uncertainty.

In that moment Mason and Blakeslee became intertwined not just physically but also emotionally. Their union, though unconventional, burned bright.

And for it they may die.

They were beaten with branches...

Their minds couldn't understand and wrap around what was happening. They were whipped

By T. STYLES

and it felt like stinging slits eating into their skin. The men whipped them on their legs.

Their backs.

And even their faces.

And when they were done, Joey, Spacey, and Minnesota huddled together in the dark room, their bodies battered and bruised from the merciless attack. The not knowing suffocated them because they didn't understand. They simply couldn't understand what Ace was doing.

"This nigga gotta go," Spacey said through clenched teeth.

"Bruh...you not fucking lying," Joey said.

"None of this made sense. He acted like we kept him in the basement while the rest of us were the evil stepsisters."

Suddenly Minnesota broke out into heavy crying.

Concerned, Spacey immediately grabbed her closer and she fell into his arms. "What is he doing?" She sobbed. "What is he doing to us?"

The room seemed to close in on them, its walls cloaked in darkness that whispered secrets of pain and suffering. "I don't know, sis," Spacey said. "I swear to God I don't."

"And at this point it doesn't even matter." Joey added.

"You ain't lying."

Minnesota was beside herself with rage. "It matters to me! I can't go through this too much longer."

"I want you both to hear me and hear me clearly..." Joey, his voice tinged with determination, was serious. "They will not break us."

"Nigga, they just whooped our asses!" Spacey said. "With branches!"

"And you alive!"

"For how long?"

"I don't know." Joey yelled. "None of us do. But despite them starving us and whipping us, we still breathing. So we can still fight."

He was trying to urge Spacey and Minnesota to find the strength within themselves to fight for their lives, to rise against Ace but they wasn't feeling it one bit.

"He hates us more intensely than I ever imagined." Minnesota's quivering voice betrayed her deep-rooted fear. "It's like, I wasn't a fan, but I never did anything to him to deserve this. If anything it was—."

160   By T. STYLES

"Spacey." Joey answered.

Spacey glared. "Y'all act like I was raping the nigga!"

"It ain't about that!" He said. "You be applying too much pressure that's all."

"Look, none of us know why he a monster." Spacey said. "Not a one of us. And I'm not gonna let y'all put that on me. But what I know is this, he won't fucking win! He just won't. You don't get to be this greasy and win."

The brothers, their voices heavy, sought to comfort Minnesota and their minds.

"I'm just glad they haven't separated us," Joey sighed. "And believe it or not, I think that shows his humane side."

"Are you fucking crazy!" Spacey yelled. "He gets no credit from me! From you either!"

"You know what...I think you're right, Joey." Minnesota said. "Why is he keeping us together? Maybe he does care."

"I didn't say he cared," Joey said. "I just say he's not the complete devil that's all."

And then they went silent and glanced around.

No food.

No light.

Phones pulled from every socket.

Their lives seemed to exist on the fringes of reality, an eerie theater where they were the unpaid actors. Each sound, each movement from outside the prison became an ominous reminder that peace would not come any time soon.

As the minutes pressed on, Joey, Spacey, and Minnesota embraced the darkness that enveloped them. They steeled themselves for the battle ahead, unaware of the horrors that lay in wait.

By T. STYLES

CHAPTER TWENTY-TWO

The bankers wanted to meet with Banks for more info on the transfer...

How ironic.

The paperwork Banks had signed had not been processed because several documents were missing. And so Ace, impeccably disguised as his wealthy father, stepped into the prestigious country club, a sanctuary for the crème de la crème of society. The luxurious surroundings unfolded before him in a way that the rich not only expected but demanded.

Pristine golf courses stretched out like emerald carpets, meticulously manicured to perfection, while elegant villas nestled among lush gardens exuded an air of exclusivity.

If you had a few million you were still too poor for the club.

Only billionaires were members.

Glimpses of shimmering swimming pools and impeccably dressed guests engaging in animated conversations painted a picture as Ace, careful to keep a measured distance from the other patrons, entered with Faye on his arm.

Feeling unworthy, he kept looking down at himself.

"You look good," she whispered. "Stop messing with your suit. You're sending off red flags."

He observed her and then the women adorned in designer gowns and dazzling jewels. Their laughter mingling with the clinking of crystal glasses made Faye look right in place.

This was her scene.

For a moment he wondered how he landed her before Banks. And he reasoned he never knew who she was until now. So he had no time to feel out of his league.

As Ace navigated the expanse of the country club, he sat at a red leather booth within the restaurant where the bankers would meet him. From where he sat, he could smell the aroma of freshly cut grass mingled with the fragrant blooms of exotic flowers.

Yet his purpose extended beyond the allure of it all. He sought to secure the financial resources necessary to build a new life, one where he could escape the clutches of his past and deeds in another country.

164

In other words, he needed all that cash up out of daddy's banks.

When situated, Faye sat next to him and was poised as their guest arrived. "Mr. Blackwood and Mr. Harrington," Faye said, rising to greet them. "You both look amazing."

"You tease," Mr. Blackwood said. "It's been how many years?"

"Four."

They looked at Ace who remained silent and toward the furthest part of the booth. This was going to be an easy deception if he did right because Faye handled a lot of the electronic business. In total, they may have met Banks twice before and both times they were at the country club.

"You look young and well," Mr. Blackwood said.

"Fuck is that supposed to mean?" Ace snapped, while readjusting his shades. He was concerned he was caught.

"I would hope all great things. Did I say something wrong?"

Faye giggled. "What Banks means is that he's been having a hard time lately with a few ventures we've been trying to get finalized. So he hadn't had much sleep."

"Is that what she means?" Mr. Blackwood asked him.

Silence.

"Anyway, so how are the children?" Faye said as she went about conversing with them both, as if Ace wasn't even in the building.

She effortlessly navigated the conversation with poise and charisma. Her words weaving an enchanting spell that solidified the lie they were selling.

Ace would get in the conversation every now and again no doubt, but they were not the same. And as a result, he couldn't shake the unease that accompanied her increasing control, a reminder that even in this world of privilege, power could be wrestled away by anyone.

Especially Faye Wales.

"Well, I was hoping we could visit your vacation home in Brazil." Mr. Blackwood said. "On that private plane of course."

"Say no more." He paused. "But I need the bank to be ready to do what I'm asking when we get there. I need things transferred to my son."

"Everything will work out."

"Everything had better work out," Ace said stronger.

166

Faye put a hand on his knee under the table because his agitation was showing. "Well, gentlemen, we will call you when it's time to take flight." She said. "Let's say, in two days?"

"We will be packed and ready."

They rose and shook Ace's hand, careful once again to look at how young he appeared.

"I'll be in contact," Ace said.

They walked away, leaving them alone. "They think they can use me, Faye," Ace said through clenched teeth, his voice filled with resentment. "They want to enjoy the privileges and perks before doing what need be done. Them niggas know I'm not my father."

A heavy silence settled between them.

"So what? If it's true it's all a part of it, Banks. Let it ride."

He looked at her hard, as if seeing her for the first time. "You're very good at this shit," he said sarcastically.

"I was born for this moment. I was born to help you."

"I bet." He walked away and she quickly followed.

The real Banks fell asleep by accident...

He had been up so many hours, that slumber came like a thief. As terrible as his nightmares were, he wished he hadn't closed his lids at all.

He saw blood.

He saw fire.

He saw death.

As his eyes adjusted to the dark room, a figure emerged from the shadows—the man he had spoken to earlier, the one who had hinted at his willingness to help without words, was inside.

Banks sat up. "Are my kids okay?"

"I don't know."

"Then what do you want?"

"I want to talk about what you mentioned the last time we saw each other." A glimmer of hope flickered within Banks as he realized that this stranger had given real thought to the moment.

"I'm listening."

"I'll help."

168   By T. STYLES

Banks nodded, doing his best to not appear too excited. "How much of the plan are you aware of from my son?"

"To be honest I don't think there is a plan." He admitted. "Not a real one anyway. And I'm gauging this by the men involved."

Banks wasn't surprised.

"So tell me what you do know."

In a hushed tone, Domingo revealed the true scale of the operation keeping Banks and his family captive on the top floor. Banks listened intently as the details unfolded, each piece of information driving home the gravity of their situation. His son, his blood, had created a plan so rusty, it made no sense that he thought things would work.

"It's a good thing you came to me. What Ace is doing is bad business. Because even if he kills me, he's leaving too many trails. He will get caught."

"With all due respect, I need more than that, sir. I need a plan."

"I been planning since I been in here. And this is what we're going to do." Banks shared the details with the man. It was a risky endeavor to trust him, requiring careful execution and courage.

When the man seemed scared Banks spoke life into him and reminded him that great things go down by average men. And that whether he knew it or not, he could do this if he was strong.

"But Ace hired killers. Paulo's men are dangerous."

"So am I." Banks said firmer. "And I'm older. Smarter. And my entire family is in this building. Who do you think you should put your trust in?"

Silence.

As minutes passed, he entrusted the stranger with more of his vision, knowing that their shared interest in escaping the clutches of Ace and Paulo would be dangerous but worth it in the end.

"I got it," Domingo said. "I'll get more information on who's who and where. And I'll bring the information to you."

"Can you confide in anyone?"

"I got three men I can trust in the world. One is not in this hotel or a part of this plan, so I've had to keep it a secret."

"You'll need the two who are here. Marcus was alone and made mistakes. That will not be you."

"You're right."

Before sealing their pact, Banks requested a favor. "I need something else." His voice revealed his deepest longing—a plea that resonated with Domingo.

"You want to do this now?"

"Yes. Right now."

"But if I fuck this up everything else will be ruined."

"Then don't fuck it up. But I need this shit. I need what I'm asking you."

The room, filled with silence, seemed to hold its breath as the weight of his answer hung heavy in the air.

They locked eyes.

"Okay."

"Thank you, brother." Their unspoken agreement, a test of loyalty, would either cement their alliance or shatter it completely.

Time would tell.

CHAPTER TWENTY-THREE

Arbella was fast asleep when Ace entered. Gripping the sheets in a bunch, she shielded her body as if he didn't know each curve. As if he hadn't looked at her flesh under soft light as she was asleep. As if he hadn't tasted every inch of her skin with his tongue, to ensure she was real.

There was no need to hide. But she did it all the same.

He entered deeper.

"What is it?" She paused. "Am I free?"

He approached her cautiously, aware of the pain he had caused and the fractured trust that hung between them. With a voice laced with sincerity, he said, "I went too far, baby. And I'm sorry."

"What does that mean?" She sat up in bed, her back against the headboard.

"It means my plans should never have excluded you. And I'm fucked up out here. I'm fucked up because I ain't got nobody I can trust."

She stood up and moved near the window.

"What about Faye?"

"Fuck that bitch!"

It was the first smile he'd seen from her in days. But just that quickly it vanished. If he wanted her back, he would have to do more. What that more was, was not her problem.

"You hurt me in ways I don't think we can come back from, Ace."

He moved closer, backing her against a wall while also not touching her body to offer respect. Not touching her flesh. Not until she gave him a full pardon.

"You hurt me so much my heart ain't beating right, Ace. How could you do this shit to me?"

He looked down.

He was so close he could smell the oil on her skin. The shampoo in her hair. He wanted to touch her. Just a little.

Arbella, her eyes brimming with vulnerability, finally looked at Ace closer. She could tell he was remorseful but even killers felt bad *the one time*.

"I'm in danger. Faye got a plan of her own. I can feel it in my heart."

She nodded. "What made you change your mind?"

"I...I was at this meeting with the bankers and—."

"And what?"

"And she didn't move right."

"So she fumbled?"

"Nah...she was perfect. Too perfect."

Arbella glared.

"Too great. And I wondered how could she be so good...so light...knowing her nigga is held hostage. Knowing what my plans for him involve."

The weight of their shared history and the wounds inflicted upon her heart lingered in the air. She listened to his words, grappling with the conflict of how much he loved her and not having her freedom.

"She's a snake."

"So are we," she said.

"But at least we're the same kind." Ace said, his voice tinged with distrust of Faye. He warned Arbella of the inherent danger of placing his trust in a woman who would choose him over her own husband.

"You doing a lot of talking." Arbella said unconvinced.

"Bring her in!" He yelled.

Suddenly Faye was brought into the room and the door was shut.

"Ace, what is this about?" Faye said, looking at him and then Arbella. "Why am I here?"

The tension in the air grew thick.

Their eyes locked, the unspoken understanding between them hanging heavy. It was a moment of reckoning, where the lines of their twisted charade were drawn, and choices had to be made.

That moment.

That night.

"Ace, what is going on?" Faye wept. "Can you talk to me please?"

"This not working."

She nodded, her legs growing weak. "Okay...okay so what does that mean? Huh? For me. Because from what I see you still need my help."

"No...I don't."

"You don't have the money transferred yet. You don't have the bankers and you were bad today. Had I not been there you would've fucked up!"

"I was." He walked closer. "I was really bad."

"So. Then what do you plan to do?" She pleaded. "Huh? You can't get rid of me! You just can't!"

"It's over," Arbella said gently from across the room.

"I stopped Walid." She blurted out.

He glared. "What you talking about?"

"I knew Walid was coming to the hotel, and I stopped him from coming to the resort. I called him, with my voice disguised and steered him away."

Ace was incensed. "When did you do this?"

"On the day you took everyone hostage. So...don't you see? You still need me."

Arbella glared. "I told you she was not to be trusted."

In that room, the fragile bonds of loyalty and love were severed, leaving behind a bittersweet aftermath. He walked up to her, moved behind her, and put his hand on her throat. From his position, he could see Arbella across the room as he held Faye's warm neck in his grasp.

Whispering in her ear he said, "I'm sorry."

He slit her throat.

Her eyes widened as she grabbed at the wound, hoping to close it back. Slowly he kneeled down by her and when she was dead, pressed his fingertips upon her lids. When it was done, and the echoes of the murder reverberated through the room, Ace and Arbella found themselves drawn together once more.

176

It was a moment devoid of trust but fueled by a desperate need to reclaim what they had on the streets. What they had before all this extra money shit got into their heads.

Arbella walked up to him, and he snatched her closer with the bloody hand. For the first time in days, with Faye's body on the floor, she jumped up on him, her legs hanging at his sides.

And he caught her.

His dick rock hard, her pussy soaking wet, he stabbed into her smoothly until the entire shaft was warm. With Arbella's back against the wall, he pumped in and out of her slowly. There was no need to rush and then it began to feel too good. So the thrusts grew quick.

Hard and passionate.

Before long, their lips met as they tried to suck the life out of one another.

They were monsters of a kind.

And they didn't care who knew.

In the aftermath of their reunion, the room became alive with their moans. The future was blurry as a bitch, but that moment was real. Only time would tell if their bond would endure what was coming next.

"If she made the call, we have to leave now," Arbella said, her lips against his. "It's just a matter of time before they find us."

"You're right. I'll call the bankers."

By T. STYLES

CHAPTER TWENTY-FOUR

The warm water soothed them...

Hours and hours of fucking was the only thing that they could do, and so they partook of it like the world was coming to an end. And afterwards, they decided to take a shower to enjoy each other more.

Was this still wrong?

Mason couldn't call it nor was he trying to at the moment. The lines were too blurred. Besides, in his mind they were going to die and so they may as well go out in orgasms.

As the liquid cascaded over their bodies, Mason and Blakeslee relished in the brief break from their confined reality. The shower offered a sanctuary, a fleeting moment of intimacy amidst the chaos that enveloped their lives.

"You can't tell me you don't love this," she said looking up at him. "You can't because if you did, I wouldn't believe you."

"You talk too much."

She giggled. "You used to love talking before—"

"Before what?"

"Before I gave you my body."

He shook his head. "You dangerous."

"And you from Baltimore. Right?"

He chuckled. "Fuck is that supposed to mean? You were never raised there. What would you know about my city?"

"I read up on you. I read up on your father. I saw how you were all deep in the streets and—."

"What does that have to do with being here? And danger."

"Being with me is dangerous and so I want to remind you that it's in your bloodline." She put a warm hand over his chest. "And in your heart." She moved her fingers there.

He shook his head.

To be so young she was good.

But their tranquility was shattered when the sound of approaching footsteps echoed toward the bathroom.

"You hear something?" She asked, turning off the water.

"Yeah! Get dressed!"

But before they could hide themselves, two men burst inside, their presence jolting Mason and Blakeslee out of their momentary escape. "Fuck do

180   By T. STYLES

you want!" He yelled at them. "And don't hurt her! You hear me, don't fucking hurt her!" Fear gripped their hearts, their naked state laid bare before the strangers who had invaded their intimate space.

"Let's go! Now!" One of the men yelled.

They snatched at the towels, covering their bodies, and were immediately escorted out of the room, the cool air drying them quick as they rushed down the hall, with their senses on high alert.

"What's going on?" Mason barked, unwilling to play the victim. If they were gonna shoot him, get it over with, was his frame of thinking.

But they ignored him as they both were led to another room. Now they found themselves confined once again, the four walls serving as a reminder that the strangers would do with them what they pleased.

"Mason, I'm scared," she admitted.

He looked down at her and pulled her close. "I can't promise what will happen, but I will die trying to save you."

It was the most romantic and yet scariest thing she ever heard in her life.

Anxiety coursed through their veins as they anxiously awaited the unknown. The two men weren't about shit. They wouldn't give up what was happening, just stared at them with probing eyes.

The atmosphere in the room was heavy with silence, punched only by the whispers of the armed men amongst themselves. Time seemed to stretch as the tension hung thick in the air.

Suddenly she was emboldened. "Does my brother know you have me in here?" She asked the men. "Does Ace know?"

"You better hope not," they finally responded.

What was that supposed to mean? Wasn't this all about Ace? Weren't all orders going straight through him?

"Fuck does that mean?" Mason questioned.

Silence.

"Does Ace know about this shit or not?" He said louder.

They ignored him.

Instead Mason and Blakeslee exchanged worried glances; their unspoken fears mirrored in their eyes. Together, they braced themselves for what lay ahead.

This very well could be the end.

An hour later, a wave of relief washed over them when they saw Banks entering with Domingo.

Mason, overcome with emotion, rushed into Banks' outstretched arms, his towel momentarily dropped before he pulled it up quickly. As they embraced, it was clear that these two loved each other harder than possibly anyone alive.

"Banks, you're safe!" He said, letting him go momentarily to tighten up the towel. "You okay? And who are these niggas?"

"Friends of Domingo's. They're solid." He paused. "But are you okay?"

"Shit rough but I'm good." Mason admitted.

Blakeslee, more reserved but no less relieved, broke between the men and offered a light hug to Banks before darting behind Mason for safety.

But what could be safer than her father?

Banks noticed the flicker of hesitation in Blakeslee's actions, a subtle indication that something weighed on her mind. "Are you okay, Blakeslee?"

She nodded. "Y...yes, father."

THE GODS OF EVERYTHING ELSE 4   183

Concern etched across his features; Banks addressed the unspoken tension. "I know you're scared." He looked at her and then Mason. "Both of you, but these men are with Domingo and—."

"Save the details," Mason said, cutting him off.

Because whatever plan he had Mason wanted it to go through without issues. And although Blakeslee's pussy was proper, she was connected to Ace which made her part-snitch.

"Okay," Banks nodded, now focusing on one fact.

They were both wearing towels.

"They didn't let you get dressed?" Banks questioned.

Mason's stomach dropped. "I had just gotten out of the shower, and she went in after me. So we didn't have time to get dressed."

One of the armed men laughed and Mason looked at him with that Baltimore killer gaze. If the man wanted to die Mason was certain he could murder one before Banks later took his life.

"What's funny?" Banks asked.

"Nothing, sir," he said in Spanish.

Banks nodded and focused on Mason and Blakeslee again. Something felt off. His heart hurt but he didn't know why.

184

Were they?

Could they be...

Fucking?

Nah, Mason would never.

"Stand by, I'll be back later and hopefully we can put all of this to an end," Banks said, hugging them both.

"I love you, man," Mason said.

"More than life," Banks replied before being taken out of the room.

CHAPTER TWENTY-FIVE

As Spacey, Minnesota, and Joey sat in the dark room, their bodies still throbbed with the remnants of the weird ass brutal beating with branches they had endured.

Shit was just crazy.

Not adding up.

And then he came. Paulo's drunk with power ass. "How are you?" He asked them.

"This nigga here..." Spacey said under his breath.

Say what you wanted, Spacey was gonna talk his shit. And sure it got him punched out more than what may have been necessary. Still, he didn't care. If he was gonna die, he was gonna die with his mouth open.

"I'm asking for real, friend," Paulo said with a hand on his chest, next to his own throat. "How are you all?"

"Man, what do you want?" Minnesota asked through clenched teeth.

"I come bearing food." He looked behind him and nodded.

By T. STYLES

Their eyes widened.

"For real?" Minnesota said.

Suddenly the most luscious meal they had since they had been there was brought in. We talking chicken, fruit, bread, liquor and even ice.

Without a second thought, they voraciously devoured anything they could touch, their minds clouded by a desperate need to get back to their strength.

They ate everything.

Even shit that wasn't edible like the rinds of lemons.

After a moment of extreme gluttony it was Spacey who knew something was wrong first. "Hold up...hold up...hold the fuck up!"

"What nigga?" Joey said.

"Something off! What you...what you..." Spacey couldn't even finish his statement. His body felt as heavy as the fine big girl he fucked a year back who he let sit on his face.

It wasn't just him who was feeling the effects.

A sense of drowsiness washed over them all, their eyelids growing heavy with each passing moment.

"They...they drugged us."

It dawned upon them, too late, that the food had been laced with a potent sedative. Panic surged within them as the realization followed—they had run themselves under a bus.

And then Ace walked inside.

Their brother.

A sharer of the Wales name.

He was wearing black slacks and a black shirt buttoned down just right. He looked like their father which was fucking them up because he was anything but the man they loved.

"You greedy ass niggas." His words, laden with cruelty and a chilling disregard for their lives, pierced through the haze of their drug-induced stupor. "I thought y'all were so smart. I thought y'all knew everything." He looked at Spacey. "Especially you."

The room spun around them, their thoughts muddled and their bodies sluggish, as they struggled to comprehend the gravity of Ace's words.

"You still a bitch!" Spacey was able to let out with all of the energy he had left.

"Facts!" Joey said in a weak tone.

"Y'all about to die. Choose the words you say to me carefully."

188   By T. STYLES

"But...we...your..." Minnesota couldn't finish talking.

Her eyes shut upon hearing the scariest words said to a human.

Y'all about to die.

As the drugs took their full effect, sleep enveloped them, dragging them into a restless slumber while their bodies lay motionless.

Soon after, they were snatched out with no fucking problem.

As Spacey, Minnesota, and Joey slowly regained consciousness, their surroundings came into focus, revealing some more bullshit. They were seated on a floor with so many spiders it was best to just stop fighting because the insects would have their way.

They found themselves in the depths of the Belizean jungle, confined within the walls of a dilapidated wooden shed. The man who was in charge of their captivity loomed before them, his words dripping with a chilling finality. He had a shotgun but how many bullets could he push out before they bit his face off?

"Where my...where my brother nigga?" Spacey asked. "Huh?"

"I thought you not like him." The man said with broken English.

"I don't, but where is he?"

"Trust me when I say it matters not," he said.

Although fear coursed through their veins, a determination burned bright within their eyes as they faced one another.

It was time to fight.

And fight hard.

Truth be told it was three on one.

But for now, they remained calm, suppressing the rage.

"I think I should be fair and let you know that you die here." He was having too much fun as he giggled. "So think of this as place where rich ass niggers die."

"Did this mothafucka just say, nigger?" Spacey snapped.

Joey put his leg on his brother. "Easy." He focused on the man. "We hear you boss. We hear you."

"Since you talking, what was the purpose of beating us with branches?" Spacey questioned.

"If they find you, which they won't, it look like you went through jungle trying to find way out. And that the bushes and brush ripped at your skin. It also look like you starved and not having eaten very much. Again, that's if they find you which they won't."

At that moment, their minds whirled with thoughts of strategy, of ways to turn the tables on his ass. Using only their vision, they looked at various parts of their captor, the shed and even each other.

A silent pact they shared, a bond that transcended words, born out of the need to live.

Sure the jungle loomed beyond the walls, its secrets and dangers awaiting them. But it was whatever at that point.

They were ready to die fighting.

So that's what the fuck they would have to do.

CHAPTER TWENTY-SIX

Tia had cooked so much food at this point for Walid, Dominik, and friends that her fingers throbbed.

But Walid gave her enough money to care for her worries for years. So she didn't mind. In fact it was relaxing having her niece, Walid, and Dominik's crew in her home. They may have been from the slums, but they were respectful because their conditions didn't describe their hearts.

They put toilet seats down.

Took out trash and anything else she needed.

At the end of the day her home was the sanctuary necessary to get down to some serious shit. Like now. And as Walid stood before Dominik's crew, a determined glint in his eyes as he addressed them with a sense of urgency. He let all know who was in charge.

"I appreciate you, Dominik," Walid said seriously. "All of you. And I'm gonna make sure you and your people good for the rest of your lives."

"My brother, you already have done that!" Dominik admitted. "My mother quit her job because the paper you gave put her good for years. Now we just wanna make sure you get that same relief. So what's the plan?"

Walid nodded in honor. "Based on the info gathered, this is the hotel where they got my family." He gave them a sheet of paper.

"I agree, brother," Dominik nodded. "The entire top floor is booked. I even had my brother Raul try to get a room for the view and he was told basically to get the fuck. That means the top floor is not available."

With a steely resolve, Walid posed the question that hung heavy in the air. "Are you ready...for you and your people to do what's necessary to help me?"

The crew exchanged determined looks, their loyalty to Dominik and their respect for the young king was littered through their expressions. "We ready." Each member of the crew, seasoned and battle-tested, nodded in affirmation.

"Good, because I can't do it without you. And I can't say everyone involved will be safe. But the Wales Warranty is this, everyone who helps, who survives, will have their lives changed for the better. I put that on my heart."

Dominik nodded and shook his hand starting at the elbow. "That's good enough for me." He looked at his men. "LET'S GO!"

Walid had settled on Ocean Lane Resorts...

It was the place his family was hidden; he was certain.

As Walid's secret crew, consisting of Dominik, his men, and the workers, stealthily moved through the hotel's corridors, their hearts pounded with the gravity of their mission.

They heard tale about Ace.

He was a madman.

And those who chose against him may meet early graves.

But they had credentials, key cards and uniforms from people actually employed for the hotel, who wanted a come up. It was easy when they learned that others who assisted, were living better for it. Disguised as housekeepers and employees, they meticulously performed their duties. With each room they cleaned, their senses sharpened, seeking any signs or clues that would lead them closer to the truth.

Was Banks and his family inside the resort?

Would Banks appreciate the trouble that went into finding him? Because trouble was heavy.

Still, the upper floor...the secret floor loomed before them, a realm of mystery and danger. And the "housekeepers" approached it with apprehension, fully aware of the risks they were undertaking.

They were now on the top floor.

Where were the men they heard stood next to the elevators because from their view they were nowhere to be found.

Every step was calculated, every breath measured, as they navigated the treacherous path that lay ahead. After hours of looking and coming up short, most were getting annoyed.

Suddenly they heard hearty laughter from men in one room. And the rest looked at one another in fear. They found the lair.

And then a real soldier presented herself.

One of the housekeepers, with nerves of steel, walked up to a room occupied by Ace's security guards on account of hearing "voices" inside. "I'm going in." The others warned her against such a move. After all, she had the main key card.

Her name was Reseda. If they were there, she wanted things to push off and she was ready for whatever. When she tapped the key and pushed open the door, time seemed to freeze as their eyes locked, the air thick with tension.

They were all sitting on the floor, bed and table talking, drinking, and getting high.

They looked greatly under the influence.

"What are you doing up here!" One man yelled, rising to his feet, before falling back down. "This is occupied! This whole floor is occupied. No cleaning up here at all."

With quick thinking, the housekeeper played the role of a lost and confused employee, masking her true intentions behind a facade of innocence. "Oh...I'm sorry...I didn't know. I didn't know."

Instead of leaving right away she remembered the face of every man present. While backing out she counted seven.

And that was all she needed.

"Close the fucking door!"

She quickly obeyed.

Her heart raced as she skillfully extricated herself from the room, leaving the guards none the

By T. STYLES

wiser. The near miss served as a chilling reminder of the dangers that lurked.

"Woman, are you crazy?" One housekeeper asked. "We were supposed to tell Dominik and 'em when we saw or heard something. Not enter ourselves."

"I'm not crazy...I just wanna new life for my family," Reseda responded. "And you should want the same. Otherwise why are we here? Now let's check the other rooms."

With renewed focus, they pushed forward, their senses heightened, ready to uncover the secrets that lay hidden within the highest floor. Led by Reseda, their perseverance paid off as they reached another room. When they pushed the door open, they were due for a surprise. Because this one was occupied by the king himself.

Banks Wales.

Standing with the door open she swallowed the lump in her throat. "Sir, are you...are you Mr. Wales?"

"Yes."

She touched her chest in relief. "Are you okay?"

He rose and he was much smaller than he had been in the past due to fewer meals. "Who are you?"

"I am Reseda. And I'm with your son Walid."

A slow smile crept up on his face. "Come inside, please. Before anyone sees you."

They followed his direction.

The air crackled with tension as they revealed their true identities, a sense of relief washing over Banks' face. In that moment, they became more than strangers brought together by a common goal—they became a united force.

"Where is my son? Is he well?"

"He's here. Somewhere." She assured him as the other housekeepers watched the meeting. "Looking for you."

Banks was grateful.

Ace may have been from hell, but Walid was all things good.

"Tell me what you know," Banks said.

The crew, understanding the significance of the information they possessed, divulged the whereabouts of the security guards who unknowingly held the key to their further progress. She spoke of room 1306 where they were all posted up. Banks, a strategic mastermind, had already linked up with Domingo to put a little something in the drinks the men had to knock them out until he could find his family.

198

And so his plan was to get Ace's men drunk and wait so that he could search the resort for his lineage. So with Walid's help things were coming together even better.

The alliance between Walid's crew and Banks solidified. Even Domingo who entered while they were speaking, having already picked Banks' side, was relieved that there was now help.

It was time for the next level.

There was still work to be done.

CHAPTER TWENTY-SEVEN

Alone again, Mason looked at Blakeslee as if she had shit on her face. It wasn't that he didn't understand that he was just as guilty for taking advantage of her body. But in his heart, he felt like she wanted Banks to find out, even if he did warn her that if Banks became aware, all bets between them would be off.

"You couldn't have faked it better when you saw him?" He asked, while seated on the chair next to the desk.

"You mean lie better?" She laid on her side and looked over at him.

"Yes! I mean lie fucking better!"

She shrugged. "I did my best."

"But you didn't though." He saw then that she was willing to risk Mason and Banks' bond, but he was not. "If he's out of the picture, in the slightest, there is no me or you."

"I don't get it."

"Except you do," he said.

She swallowed. "So if Banks cut you off, you gonna cut—."

"He's your father. Call it what it is."

"Right now he's not. Right now he's the woman who's coming in between something and somebody I want. If you don't see that you are crazier than I thought."

He glared. "Don't disrespect him again."

"I'm sorry I--."

"Sorrows do nothing for a nigga like me."

"Yet it is all I offer," she said firmly. "I told you what I wanted. Haven't you wanted something so badly you were willing to risk it all?"

Silence.

She saw in his eyes the answer was yes. "My father...that's how you felt about him?"

"There is no world with me where he doesn't exist. And it's important for you to know that. So despite your jealousy or whatever else you got going on, you better start understanding that shit."

Mason and Blakeslee, their relationship strained by the weight of their circumstances, remained on opposite corners of the room. The air between them funky, the blame game in full effect.

Suddenly, the door swung open, revealing Banks accompanied by Walid's female crew. The room seemed to hold its breath as Banks stepped forward, his expression light.

"I just walked into the room and found the Triad with Sugar." Banks said happily. "They're all safe. I have a nanny and nurse checking them out but, they look well. Even gained a few pounds."

Mason breathed deeply. "The weight is lifted," Mason admitted.

"I'm so happy, father," she said, running up to Banks, hugging him tightly. She put on a show, almost too good.

Yet, relief was short-lived as he registered the absence of Spacey, Minnesota, and Joey. "What you mean you can't find them?" Mason asked. "They were here."

Sure his son, being one of the Triad members, was safe. And that felt good. But Banks' kids were important to him, especially Spacey with whom he built a strong bond.

"We don't know where they are. All we know is that they aren't in this hotel." His voice, tinged with worry, made the room heavier.

The realization that they weren't accounted for ruined the mood. Fuck were they celebrating for if Spacey and 'em were missing?

"How did you even get out?" Mason questioned.

"The guards are all high and shit in their room," Banks said.

"How you do that?" Mason grinned.

"Domingo, who's one of them, put a sedative in their drinks for me. But that shit will be wearing off soon and I got some questions to ask them."

"And Paulo?" Mason asked through clenched teeth.

"He's not with the other guards, and so far, no one has seen him. He may be wherever my children are." Banks reasoned.

Mason shook his head and stepped closer. "I don't know how but you will find Spacey and them. We will find them. Together."

Banks wanted to believe. "How can you be sure? Ace is reckless and he hates Spacey. I even saw him...I saw him put a gun to his head."

Blakeslee's jaw dropped. It was easy romanticizing gangster shit until you came in contact with a true killer.

"Because you deserved a lot of shit but losing another child ain't it, Banks. They are well, I feel it."

A sense of unity settled over the room.

"I hear you." Banks said.

"Trust me."

You see, this is why Banks fucked with him. Mason put him at ease. Some people had organs like the heart, lungs, and the liver to keep their body moving.

Banks had Mason.

It was simple.

Minnesota, Joey, and Spacey, their bodies weak but their spirits strong, looked at one another with a final nod.

They had been sizing up their captor for a moment and they did a good job too. They saw how every five minutes his eyes seemed to grow heavy. They saw how the hard seat made him uncomfortable, so he would shift every ten minutes.

Their bodies were wrecked with pain, but they remained still. They remained quiet. Reserving all energy for this moment. While also being afraid that he would get the call that would say, "Kill them".

And then Spacey looked at his siblings. It was the man's sleeping time, so they seized the

By T. STYLES

moment. All three of them, arms bound with ropes, charged him full speed.

Had the guard not been so tired he could've killed one and dealt with the aftermath later. But he allowed their nonmoving bodies to convince him that they were weak, tired, and pitiful.

Wrong move.

They managed to overpower the man. The rush of adrenaline fueled their determination. Spacey went straight with his forehead to the man's jaw. It wasn't like he wasn't the best candidate to do that shit. He had been punched in the face so much at the resort it was almost as if he were in training for that moment.

That one strong head butt had him seeing space.

And when he was out cold, they frantically searched for the keys that would unlock their freedom. I mean he had to get them in the jungle some way, right? They wouldn't just drop him off with no way to get home.

Where are the keys, bitch?

Was the motto.

With each passing moment, their hope grew, the taste of liberation tantalizingly close. "Got 'em!"

Spacey said, face bleeding from that head-crack-head-crack.

"Nigga, you good for something after all!" Joey admitted.

After finding a knife on the man's hip, they cut off their ropes. First Spacey held the knife close behind his back and each sibling turned around and had their threads sawed. And when they were free, Joey cut Spacey's.

"Let's get the fuck out of here!" Joey said, rubbing his wrists.

They escaped the shed and looked for the ride. Nothing.

Where was it? They all thought.

Their elation was short-lived as they realized that the man's vehicle was nowhere to be found. Panic set in as they grappled with being stranded in the depths of the unforgiving jungle. Their escape, once within reach, now seemed impossible.

As despair threatened to take hold of their minds, rain descended upon the jungle. The powerful storm raged and mirrored everything going wrong. Torrents of water cascaded from the heavens, turning everything into mud.

By T. STYLES

"I don't believe this shit," was all Spacey could say. "Why can't we catch a break?"

Minnesota cried but one could not tell because the rain was relentless as it pounded upon her face.

It soaked their clothes and obscured their vision. Each step became a battle. And then the wind got involved. Slapping the fuck out of them as they tried to find shelter.

Their escape plan came up short.

Their progress slowed.

"Let's not give up!" Joey said, looking at them. He extended his hand and Minnesota locked in first, and Spacey grabbed her hand. Now they were a human chain.

They pushed.

The rain-soaked ground threatened to swallow their every step. Yet, their determination burned bright, refusing to go out.

The deafening roar of thunder and the blinding flashes of lightning didn't stop them. As the rain washed down upon them, their spirits remained unbroken.

They were united.

Locked in.

It was the Wales Warranty that they could last
no matter what.

And so they lived up to the calling.

CHAPTER TWENTY-EIGHT

As Ace's men begin to awaken from a thick sleep, they realized one of their own had yet to return after checking on Banks. Where was he?

"I'll go see what's up."

"Good cause I'm still out of it," they said, their guts busy with whiskey, vodka and rum supplied by Ace.

As the guard from room 1306 ventured out, his footsteps echoing through the dimly lit corridor, he knew not what danger lurked around the corner.

Domingo, ever watchful and determined, seized the opportunity. "You good?" Domingo asked.

The man frowned, turned around and swayed. Still fucked up off the tainted drink. "Am I good? Where were you?"

"I was seeing about Banks."

"What you find out?"

"This!" With a swift and precise blow to the face, Domingo incapacitated the unsuspecting guard, a prior friend, rendering him unconscious. This happened just as he saw his brother Dominik walking down the hall.

Since they hadn't talked about him coming to the hotel Domingo was confused. "Wait...who you with?" Dominik asked.

"Who you with, brother?"

Silence kept them steady for a moment.

"I was working with Ace, but I switched up. What about you?"

"How you get tied in with Ace?" Dominik questioned.

"It doesn't even matter now. What are you doing though?"

"I'm helping Walid," Dominik admitted. "And I'm glad you changed your mind because that nigga is going down. I think he left at the last minute, leaving these niggas alone but I don't know why."

Blood on blood, they were resolute in his mission to help Walid and his family. The connection came just as Walid was walking up in the hallway. "Who is your friend?" Walid questioned Dominik.

"My brother. And from what I hear, a brother to you too."

"How you figure?"

"He's helping your father."

Walid grinned. "Good. Come with me."

The brothers followed.

Using a key card he accessed a room which held another guard who ventured down to check on his father earlier, only to find Walid instead. Despite shit coming together, he had yet to find his father or Mason.

"We have company," Walid announced.

All three walked inside.

Walid, his voice calm yet firm, leaned over the caught guard, his eyes piercing black. With unwavering resolve, he said, "Where the fuck is my family? Because I can tell they were in this room."

"Your siblings were here. Like I told you when you found me. I don't know where they are now."

"What about my father?"

"I moved him to see Mason earlier, but I don't know where he is now," Domingo interjected. "But I got a feeling he was checking on everybody else, since word is Ace is gone."

It wasn't good enough for Walid.

"What do you know?" He asked the caught guard.

The room fell into an intense silence, each breath held in anticipation.

With a groan, the guard said, "I don't know about your father. But Ace is about to board a plane."

Walid backed up.

Angry.

"I need more. Leave nothing out!" Walid demanded.

The guard began to divulge the names of those who had participated in Ace's nefarious plan. Each word and name that left his lips carried immense significance, unraveling the weak web of deceit Ace laid out.

"That's all I know," he promised. "But Luci, who's in 1306, knows all. You need him. Trust me."

Walid listened intently, etching each name into his memory. It was a bittersweet moment. The guard's compliance represented a crucial breakthrough.

Walid was right.

This was the right hotel.

This was the right spot.

But where was his family?

Suddenly Walid smiled as he received a message that changed everything. "Keep him right here, Dominik. I know where my father is." He rushed out.

212　**By T. STYLES**

As Banks stepped into the room, his eyes immediately locked onto the figure of his long-lost son, Walid. The weight of uncertainty lifted from his shoulders, replaced by an overwhelming surge of relief. Emotion coursed through him, rendering him momentarily speechless.

"Father," he said, rushing up to him, locking him in a strong embrace. "Where is pops?"

"He's fine," he promised. "For now he's fine."

A smile tugged at the corners of Banks' lips, his eyes sparkling with unshed tears. The sight of his son, standing tall and strong, filled him with an indescribable sense of pride. In that instant, the bond between father and son transcended time and erased all he'd been through over the 12 days.

To be reunited with Walid, to witness his strength and selflessness firsthand, was a gift beyond measure. Especially with Ace being out there just wrong.

"We aren't done yet though, son," Banks admitted. "We gotta find Spacey and them too."

He gave him the details.

CHAPTER TWENTY-NINE

"We looking good!" The Belizean pilot boasted from the cockpit. "Clear skies the entire ride!"

As if it ruled the air, the sexy black private jet soared, its sleek exterior reflecting the yellow hues of the setting sun. The word WALES in silver plastered across both sides let the lessers know which billionaire owned the world.

Of course it was Banks Wales!

Or so they thought.

Playing the role of Banks, Ace Wales, a man of mystery and charm, reclined in the cocaine white plush leather seat, his tailored black suit accentuating his impeccable style. The smoked colored 24k gold shades made it difficult to see he was on his imposter shit, because his eyes were hidden behind expensive ombre lenses.

By his side, his breathtakingly beautiful woman, Arbella was propped and ready for show. Sure she wasn't Banks' wife, Faye Wales. But what wealthy man you knew didn't have a little something younger on the side? Her long flowing hair cascading downward like a black waterfall around her delicate chocolate features made her look unreal.

She was bad for sure and yet her eyes laid heavy with the troubles of this trip. But she had better not show it because her fear, her worry, could ruin it all.

They were entertaining two bankers, hoping that they would buy what Ace was selling and do what he wanted. To transfer all money and assets from Banks to his son, Ace Wales.

Yep, for the evening Ace had taken over his father's persona and Arbella was a willing and sexy accomplice. The bankers legit assumed that it was the king who was taking the meeting because Ace was back on his old shit.

Greed.

Treachery.

Deceit.

To his family, he had proven that he would forever be a monster who would do everything he could to not only live like his father but become his father.

And yet something felt off to the guests.

In the spacious cabin, Mr. Blackwood and Mr. Harrington nervously exchanged glances at one

216   **By T. STYLES**

another. They had met Mr. Wales briefly only two other times in person, so they were somewhat confused. Normally Faye conducted all business face to face. Because Banks couldn't be bothered. He was running too many businesses. He would simply log on and see that what he expected was reflected in his banking accounts.

Each time it was.

So this was different.

Still, if the man before them was the great Banks Wales, who was up in age, the years did him well. Like he could bottle what he was taking because he looked so fucking good.

Don't get it twisted.

Ace moved like Banks.

Sounded like Banks.

But he was not Banks.

He practiced for months before making the switch. And since he was his son, the features he possessed made it easier for those to believe who wanted to believe the lie. He even went all out to have gray hair that was kept in a low curly $300 haircut. But where were the wrinkles? Where were the soft crinkling of the skin on the hands that indicated age had visited and within near time death would follow?

"So I expect you have everything you need to transfer my funds to my son when it's time?" Ace said in his best daddy 'War-Banks' voice. "Like I mentioned I haven't been feeling well and I want to ensure all funds are in order if anything happens to me."

"Of course," Mr. Blackwood nodded. "Although we're unsure why you wouldn't get your lawyers involved."

"Mainly because they handle things when I'm dead." He took a sip and dusted invisible lint off his clothes. "But as you both can see, a nigga is still alive."

They cleared their throats.

"We understand," Mr. Blackwood said. "And I know you're upset about all of the hoops we made you jump through. But we needed to make sure you know..."

"No, I don't know."

"What my colleague is saying is that...well...you are leaving billions to him. Not to mention you just made a huge transfer to Mason Louisville. So we want to make sure that you are...well."

Earlier that month to make sure Mason knew that he cared for him and his legacy, Banks broke off half of his funds to him. That was done with paperwork and lawyers. But when "fake Banks" wanted to do it again so soon, the bankers sounded off an alert.

And this is what sponsored the charade in the jet.

"Well, are you satisfied now?" Ace said. "That I want my wishes carried out?"

The silence was heavy.

In it held a lot. Would all benefit from the blue-sky robbery that was obviously taking place by siphoning tons under the guise of Ace being his father?

"We are satisfied," Blackwood said with a slight smile.

"Good." Ace said, on his best boss shit. "And don't worry. All of my future funds will continue to go through Blackwood & Harrington Bank. With the deal I'm closing now, it will make your institution one of the wealthiest in the world."

As the jet cruised at a dizzying altitude, suddenly Ace's focus shifted from the men to the unsettling noises coming from the cockpit. The plane rattled, the engine sputtered, and alarms blared. A growing sense of trepidation settled over the passengers as they realized something was gravely wrong.

They were falling.

Fast!

Flying back and forth like a ball in a foosball game, Ace rose and rushed into the cockpit.

What he saw next caused his heart to rattle.

The pilot was slumped forward, and he was both unconscious and unresponsive as he shook him for dear life. "Johnson, get up! Wake the fuck up!"

He didn't.

Slowly Ace backed up in fear.

"What's wrong with the pilot?" Blackwood said standing behind him. He hadn't even known he was there.

Ace looked back at him. "I...I don't know!"

"Well you're a pilot right?!" He yelled. "What are you waiting on? Fly us to safety!"

Ace looked dumb. He was out of his league and had been caught in the worst way imaginable.

He was not Banks Wales!

He would have screamed it from the rooftop if it meant safety at this point, but it was too late. They were about to die, all to appease the bankers who wanted to squeeze out a few perks to help Ace siphon money.

They were descending rapidly. So fast that they would all crash to the aqua green water within two minutes.

And suddenly the pilot woke up.

As if nothing ever happened.

His eyes widened and he quickly went into action. Seeing they were all about to meet their fate, made a few clicks in the cockpit, maneuvered the control yokes, and pulled the plane into a comfortable altitude.

But he wasn't well. Calling into the control station he said, "I have narcolepsy and I need to land now!"

Ace was furious. Out of all the pilots he got one who had a flare up during the worst time.

It was then that Ace realized they would be headed back to Belize. And it was also clear that someone may be aware when he landed that he was not who he said he was.

Feeling relieved. Mr. Blackwood returned to his seat with his colleague who was gripping his chest.

Ace sat down also and held Arbella's hand tightly. "Is there any way I can get you to transfer the funds now?" He asked Harrington, almost jokingly realizing the gig was up.

"All you can do for me is get me out of this plane!" He proceeded to whisper to his peer.

"I think we fucked up," he said in Arbella's ear.

"I know, baby. But I'm riding with you no matter what."

It was music to his ears.

By T. STYLES

CHAPTER THIRTY

As the guard, Luci, from 1306 ventured down the corridor, a sense of unease settled upon him.

Where was Domingo?

Where was Hector?

Why were his peers missing?

His footsteps echoed through the hallway. Concern etched across his face as he continued. He ain't even want no parts of this for real, for real. He had been talked into Ace's plan by his cousin Mickey's girl on his father's nephew's brother's side.

Greedy as the others he said yes.

Now to think that Ace may have left them hanging, made him sick.

Still as he moved closer to Banks' door, he took a deep breath. Then he pushed open the door to the room where Banks should be, but his heart pounded in his chest at what he saw. What awaited him inside was a sight that struck him like a bolt of lightning. There, sitting on the edge of the bed, was his own wife, her expression filled with sorrow. She was surrounded by Banks, Walid, Dominik, Domingo, and more men he didn't know.

She was in danger!

Big time!

The room seemed to shrink, the walls closing in as the weight of the moment pressed upon him. Confusion clouded his thoughts as he stared at the unexpected presence of the love of his life.

"Sweetheart, what's going on?" His head still banging from the tainted drink.

"You have to come clean."

"Come clean?" His mind raced, trying to comprehend the implications of her presence. "What...what do you mean?"

"She means we not playing with you, nigga. At all." Walid said firmly. "And you better give us some answers."

In that charged moment, he found himself torn between his duty to Ace and the love he held for his wife.

"Son, you can save yourself," Banks said. "And your wife. But you won't get another opp."

Walid and Banks watched on, their eyes focused intently on the guard, recognizing the opportunity that had presented itself would not last.

224   By T. STYLES

Would he take it?

One thing for sure was that things changed now.

"Please, husband, don't play with these people." His wife's voice trembled as she implored him to break the silence, to reveal the whereabouts of Minnesota, Spacey, and Joey.

"Where are they?" Walid pushed harder. "Where are my brothers and sister?"

"I don't...I don't know."

"You sure you wanna play these games?"

"Husband...speak! Now! Think of me. Our child and our family." Her plea, laced with fear and desperation, resonated. "They know where we live. Where we play!"

"What you gonna do?" Walid said plainly. "Because unlike the time you think you got, I don't have all day." The guard stood frozen, the weight of his decision bearing down upon him.

"Where are they?" Banks asked.

The room felt suffocating, the air thick with tension.

"It's your last opportunity."

Walid and Banks watched with bated breath; their hopes pinned on the guard's choice. Besides, the fate of Minnesota, Spacey, and Joey hung in the distance. He swallowed the lump in his throat, "Ok. I'll tell you what I know."

Relief.

By T. STYLES

CHAPTER THIRTY-ONE

After Luci's wife pleaded for him to reveal the whereabouts of Minnesota, Spacey, and Joey, he told everything he knew.

He went into detail about who was left in room 1306 but he was firm on not knowing where Spacey and 'em were. But he did mention the jungle. Still, Walid, Banks, and Dominik planned the attack. After all, the women did their part, and it was up to them to seal the deal. They had the name, address, and livelihood of every guard in the hotel room. So even if they escaped, they would await them in their homes.

"Let's go," Walid said.

"I'm going with," Banks said in the room.

"No, father. Let me do this. I got this far on my own. Let me continue."

"You sure, son?"

"Please, I don't want to worry about you."

The strength Banks had watching his son take charge made him realize that he and Mason's blood didn't mix poorly together. That maybe, just maybe they had done something right after all.

"Okay, son." Banks said with a heavy hand on his shoulder. "I'll be waiting. If I wait too long though, I'm coming looking for you."

Walid hugged him and together with Dominik, they led Luci out to room 1306. Sure they could have gotten the police involved at this point. But in Walid's opinion they were too corrupt. And it was best to handle things on his own.

When they arrived at the door Walid looked dead into his eyes. "One wrong move, you get the first bullet."

Luci nodded. "I understand."

"Go," Dominik said, his weapon trained on him.

In a swift and calculated motion, Luci opened the door and yelled, "Where is Spacey and—."

Ace's men fired.

They had been waiting.

No answers were given, at least not in the smoke.

But Walid and his men sprang into action, overpowering three of Ace's men who were struck with bullets. The other two took their shirts off ready to go to blows. The room became suddenly a battleground, as bodies dropped in what, if Walid was being honest, was light work.

Where was the fight?

228　　By T. STYLES

Where was the grunt?

At the end of the day Ace hadn't paid anybody enough to fight hard enough for him. And the foal of the takeover was lackluster.

"If you so bad, why don't you fight with your hands?" One of Ace's men said to Dominik, as he and the other got ready.

"This what you want?" Dominik replied.

Walid laughed as Dominik and Yazo got busy. Punches were thrown by the remaining men, but Walid's folks landed blow after blow with precision. Within seconds, the weight of justice tipped in Walid's favor.

In the chaos, Ace's remaining people were outnumbered.

As the dust settled, the room fell into an uneasy calm, Walid, Dominik, Yazo and Luci looked at one another, after stepping over bodies.

They were done.

But where was Spacey and 'em?

"I'm sorry," Dominik said to Walid. "Them dudes weren't talking though. We gonna find your people."

"For real," Yazo added.

In the wake of their victory, they had to deal with the fact that they had zero information on his siblings.

And the shit hurt.

He was certain that Dominik was right and that he would find them. Besides, he felt led. Like something was guiding him. And he had to be calm to hear the voice.

He just had to keep his head on.

And shit would work out.

He prayed it would.

Slowly Walid exited the room and approached his father.

"Did you find them?" Banks asked.

The look in his eyes told him he didn't. Banks felt like someone drop-kicked him. But he kept it together. For Walid. Who was taking it harder than anyone else.

Banks led Walid down the hotel hall until they reached a room where Mason awaited, anticipation etched across Walid's face. As the door swung

By T. STYLES

open, Mason's eyes locked onto Walid's form, and his heart skipped a beat.

"Son!"

"Pops!" Without hesitation, he enveloped his son in a tight embrace, holding him close as if trying to make up for lost time.

"Oh, my son," Mason whispered, his voice choked with emotion. "I can't express how fucking proud of you I am. Through all this shit you remained solid. Holding onto code! And you found us!"

Walid, his eyes shining with gratitude, returned the embrace, feeling the strength and love flowing between them. Mason's words resonated deep within his soul because he didn't feel strong now.

And if truth be told he needed *all dat.*

Blakeslee, her eyes brimming with tears, finally approached Walid with open arms. Their embrace was tight and tender, a shared understanding passing between siblings. But when it was over, she quickly returned to Mason's side.

Walid glared.

What was that about?

He didn't have time to analyze it. There was still work to be done.

As news of the harrowing hostage situation reached the ears of the hotel management staff, a sense of shock and disbelief washed over them.

Swiftly, the hotel management sprang into action, flooding rooms with out of towners who had nothing to do with the shit to see if anybody else was taken against their will. They found a few girls who were being trafficked and saved their lives.

It was dumb, and too late for the staff, but the Wales' let them do what they must.

In the end the staff returned with apologies, sorrows, and weak pleas. And it still would not bring back Spacey, Joey and Minnesota.

At least the Triad and Sugar are fine. And their surprise at everything going down at the hotel made the situation stranger since the young boys were clueless. Everyone else was in heaven, but they were none the wiser.

"We were taken hostage?" Bolt asked. "We thought we were just watching ourselves."

The Triad laughed at one another as Banks told them they would have to hang back a bit longer.

232 **By T. STYLES**

He stopped short of giving them more information because for real, he didn't have the energy.

He dismissed the boys.

Focusing back on the GM of the hotel he said, "I have three adult children still missing," Banks took a deep breath. "If you want to help, question your people about if they saw anything. Start there."

"Of course." Management agreed.

More apologies spilled from their lips as they pledged their full support and cooperation, vowing to help in any way possible to assist the traumatized family.

Banks, Mason, Walid, and Blakeslee were all shaken by their ordeal.

And no sleep would come until they found everyone.

And dealt with Ace once and for all.

CHAPTER THIRTY-TWO

Walid, Banks, Mason, and Blakeslee were in Banks' suite, going over next steps. Before details were given, they looked at Blakeslee like she was an alien.

"What?" She asked.

"We need the room," Banks said.

She looked at Mason and then at her father. "Okay...I'll...I'll be outside if you need me."

After Blakeslee excused herself, leaving them alone, to grapple with the weight of their impending decision, a profound silence settled upon the men. The air seemed to thicken with anticipation, as each braced himself for the difficult conversation that lay ahead.

"What of Ace?" Banks asked plainly.

Mason and Walid looked down.

"We need to talk about this, men."

"I know, father. You're right." Walid took a deep breath.

"I knew he had issues with us, but I never knew he would go this far." Banks started. "It's like it's not about the money at this point."

"It's like he's trying to destroy us," Mason said.

"Starving your own siblings?" Banks said. "What is wrong with him!"

Walid frowned. "Wait...he starved them?"

"Yes. Would feed me but that was probably to keep my mind right so I could sign over everything. But I would always throw away the main form needed."

"Or to put a weft between y'all." Walid walked over to the sofa and flopped down. "Brother, what are you doing?" He said to himself. "What are you..."

Mason walked over and put a hand on his shoulder. "This is not about you, and I don't want you to take this on."

Banks walked over and sat on his left. "You saved us. And I'll never forget this."

"But...I don't understand where the hate comes from, father. Like...why does he, why does he act like this?"

In the hushed space, the trio exchanged glances, their eyes communicating a depth of understanding that transcended words. The gravity of their situation pressed upon them, a heavy burden that demanded action, no matter how unsavory.

The nigga had gone too far.

He had always gone too far.

Did too much.

It was almost as if he wanted to die.

If that's what he wanted, so be it.

"I'll do it." Mason, his voice filled with sorrow, said softly. "I'll take care of him."

"What does that mean?" Banks said.

"You know what it means."

Unable to say the words, he expressed in one sentence his belief that Ace must pay the ultimate price.

"Do you know what that will do to you?" Banks asked. "Do you know what it will do to your soul?"

"Yes, and I also know that if you did it, you would worry about how I felt about the decision for the rest of our lives." Mason acknowledged the burden that would rest upon his shoulders, the weight of pulling the trigger. "And I can't have that."

But he took it on.

"I can't believe we gotta even talk like this," Walid said looking downward.

"Me either, son," Banks said. "Me either."

"I can handle it," Mason said. "I...I can handle it because I want his last moments to be from someone who..."

His voice trailed off.

This shit hurt.

Beyond belief.

"Someone who loves him," Mason continued.

And so, he pledged to bear the weight of that final act, sparing Banks from the burden, and ensuring their bond remained intact. It was a somber exchange, underscored by the profound love and understanding that held them together for years.

With the decision made, they sat in silence a bit more.

The Triad had knocked on the door several times begging to know more about what Ace had done, and they were sent on the way by Banks' men who now took over the entire hotel.

Best believe they were safe now.

Just as the weight of their decision settled upon them, a ringing phone shattered the solemnity of the moment.

It was Walid's cell.

"Who is it?" Banks asked.

"I don't know."

"Hello..."

"Brother, is that you!" Spacey yelled from the other end.

Walid jumped up, leaving Banks and Mason to look at him wondering what was going on.

"Are you okay?" He asked excitedly.

"Are you?!" Spacey said cheerfully, rain pounding in the background. "Ace done kidnapped us and—."

"Everything is okay now! I know what happened!"

"You saved them, didn't you?" Spacey yelled. "I knew you would! I knew you would!"

"Wait, that's Walid?" Minnesota said in the background.

"It's Spacey and them," Walid told Banks and Mason who immediately breathed deeply and exhaled.

Relief surged through Walid, Banks, and Mason in that joyous moment.

"We need help though! I'm using this nigga's phone. We found it in his car. And it's raining and we stuck in this Jeep."

"Send me your coordinates!" Walid said. "And I'll be in route!"

238   By T. STYLES

While Walid went to fetch his siblings, Banks, feeling a nagging sense of unease with Blakeslee, decided to see about her in her private room. "Can we talk?" He asked.

It was time for him to address a matter that weighed heavily on his mind. The air between them felt stiff.

"About what father?"

"First, how are you?"

"Scared."

"Of me?"

"Yes."

Banks walked deeper into the room and looked at her view of the outside. Then he looked at the bed and back at her. This was the space she shared with his best friend.

"Is there something you want to tell me?"

Blakeslee, her gaze steady yet guarded, considered her response carefully. In her heart, she held a secret—a connection with Banks' best friend, Mason—that she had chosen to keep buried deep. Besides, Mason had made himself clear.

No Banks...no them.

And that was a problem for her.

Still fear coursed through her veins, knowing the potential of exposing the truth. "Father...I...I don't know what you want."

"Blakeslee...is there something you want to tell me?" He asked firmer.

With a measured breath, Blakeslee said, "No, father."

"Then why so long to respond?"

"I don't know what you want from me. But I'm being honest, father. I have nothing to tell you at this moment."

"At this moment?"

"Yes, at this time," she said.

Banks, keenly aware of all, sensed the truth that lingered beneath Blakeslee's response. Though he wanted honesty and transparency, he would let all breathe for now.

Besides, did he really want to know the truth?

"Okay...okay..." he hugged her.

At that time, both Banks and Blakeslee recognized the fragile nature of their relationship. The path they had chosen—one of secrets and unspoken truths—was heavy.

Nothing between them would ever be the same.

By T. STYLES

Ever.

In a van with Dominik and his men, Walid embarked on his journey to retrieve Minnesota, Spacey, and Joey from their location.

"You good over there?" Dominik asked as he steered the van.

"Nah...I'm not." Walid looked out the window.

He nodded. "You gonna find your brother."

"To be honest, I don't want to."

He glared. "Why? That's what this is all about right?"

"Because there are things that will happen when I find him, Dominik."

He nodded. "How was your relationship with him? After the last time you saw him."

"Fragile. We fought."

"Wow." Dominik continued to drive.

Walid dragged a hand down his face. "I know."

"Listen, I don't know what kind of relationship you have with him, but you a real dude. And that's rare."

"You wanted to kick my ass days ago."

"Correction, I did kick your ass some days ago."

Walid laughed. "No lies."

"But I'm glad I met you. And whatever you gotta say to your brother, say it even if it may be the last time he breathes."

Amidst the winding roads and the blur of passing scenery, he thought about what he said. He hoped things would be good but what his pops was going to have to deal with by killing his brother fucked him up. He always worried for everybody he loved.

Even his evil twin.

Suddenly a high pitch ring pierced the air, signaling an incoming call. Walid's heart skipped a beat as he answered, the voice on the other end delivering news that sent shockwaves through his being.

"Your brother's touching down at this hangar!" A friend said. "Come now! Come now and we'll hold him as long as we can!"

After everything kicked off earlier in the day, Walid had men at the hangars in the event Ace showed up. And that hunch had paid off. Ace, his reckless ass brother, had been located at the airport, narrowly escaping a plane crash.

242   **By T. STYLES**

Walid was at odds.

On one hand, the prospect of Ace being within their grasp brought a sense of closure, an opportunity to confront the same nigga who plagued their lives for days. Yet, the near-miss plane crash served as a reminder of the lengths to which Ace would go to maintain his lie.

He had to call Mason and Banks.

He had to do it now!

CHAPTER THIRTY-THREE

Banks was in the room with Mason, and Mason had just removed a cell phone from his ear. "What is it, friend?"

"That was Walid," Mason said, taking a deep breath. "Ace has been found. Apparently he had men scouting all the local hangars and when a call came in about an emergency landing, he knew where he'd be."

"Smart." Banks sat down on the edge of the couch.

"Are you sure about this?" Banks, consumed by the weight of the decision, sought a final confirmation from Mason, his trusted ally.

Mason felt ill.

He had killed many people before, but this was his son. Whom he loved. And since he lost so many in the past, this decision was even heavier. Outside of Walid and Bolt, he didn't have any more children.

But one of his sons was a monster. And he was directly targeting his own family members. If he didn't deal with it now he would attack them again, and again. Which meant he had to go tonight.

In a quiet and solemn moment, he looked into Mason's eyes, searching for any sign of hesitation or doubt. "Are you gonna be okay? You gotta tell me something."

Silence.

"Mason..." He breathed deeply. "I can do it if you need me. But I don't want you to hate me for this later."

"There is no other way is there? We have to kill our child?"

"No other way, brother," Banks said in a low voice. "I love him too, but I can't rest with him roaming. I just can't. He tried to kill us."

"Again," Mason added. His gaze unwavering, met Banks' searching eyes. "I got it..."

Banks breathed deeply.

"I'll be fine." With a firm nod, he assured Banks that he was indeed certain about the path he had chosen, and that he would see it through to the end.

With a heavy heart, Banks extended his hand, their hands clasping in a final gesture of trust.

Silently, Mason turned and left the room, their conversation lingering in the air.

It was dark times.

Ace and Arbella were surrounded by Walid's men with guns in every direction when Mason reached the hangar. Yazo, one of Walid's men, accompanied Mason per Walid's request.

As Ace stood waiting, the fear he felt was written all over his face and his eyes widened as Mason's presence sent a chilling ripple through his veins when he exited the luxury van. He had already been relieved of all weapons.

"Pops," Ace said, his voice shaking. "I wasn't going to hurt any of you. I was just—."

"We heard this shit before! We heard all of this before from you! And yet it's always the same. You feel slighted so you come at all of us instead of trying to bond. We your family, nigga!"

Ace glared. "You sound like him."

"That's all you have to say? I mean look at you. You're dressed like Banks and yet you hate him so much."

Silence.

246

He was done talking.

With a command, Mason's voice was heavy when he said, "Put them both inside. It's no use."

Arbella held onto Ace's arm with all of her might. It was obvious that there was no room for negotiation or escape. Ace, Arbella by his side, got into the van.

Yazo took the driver's seat while Mason kept the passenger's seat warm.

Arbella and Ace were in back with another man behind them ready to fire if he tried to get away. Silence settled within the vehicle as they drove, the weight of Ace's fate hanging heavy in the air. Unspoken tension permeated the space, each occupant aware of the grim reality of what was about to unfold.

His ass was about to die.

He wasn't sorry enough in Mason's mind.

Instead Ace appeared cocky, arrogant, as if he himself planned his death.

With Yazo driving, Mason kept looking behind himself, at Ace who was whispering into Arbella's ear as tears streamed down her face. They were clutching each other so hard blood flow couldn't move easily through their veins.

"You should drink some water," Yazo said, handing it to Mason, also interrupting his thoughts. "I see you keep going at your lips."

Mason nodded, because he had been licking them bitches hard too. "Yeah, I been fucked up lately. Probably dehydrated too."

Mason drank the entire bottle, and when he was done suddenly, he felt sleepy. Looking over at Yazo he said, "What did you do?"

"Sorry, man," he said, under his breath. "I had to do it."

It was the last thing he heard before closing his eyes.

Yazo had owed Walid for fucking up at the brothel and the payback was giving his father a sedative to literally put him out of his misery for what was about to happen next.

Just then Walid pulled up to the van and Yazo pulled over to the side of the road as planned.

"What's going on?" Ace asked Yazo from the backseat.

"You'll find out."

Walid stepped out of his Benz, yanked at Ace's door, and said, "Get out, nigga."

"What's going on, brother?" Ace asked him.

"Everything." Walid was firm and sick of it all. "Now get the fuck out!"

Ace looked at Arbella, kissed her and held her tightly. He felt like this was the end. When he was done calming her, he eased out and faced his own face. While Yazo and his men stood on the ready to blow Ace's back out if he got shifty.

"So it's you huh?" Ace asked. "You gonna kill your own brother? Your own face."

Silence.

"Listen, man, I—."

"What did I do to make you hate us so much?" Walid asked.

Ace frowned. "You?"

"Yes...me."

Ace looked down. "Do you remember when I asked you to come to the states with me and you refused? Because I was sick of father's rules?"

Silence.

"That's when I knew you chose them over me. When I shared a womb with you. This is the result. You betrayed your twin!"

"Them? You mean our family?"

"Yes, nigga! I don't give a fuck who it is, for real! You my twin. My brother and you chose them over me! How could you do that shit?"

"You had a chance to reconnect with me! With us! And all you had to do was let your ego go. But you too greedy! Always too fucking greedy!"

Ace shook his head and looked down. "You're right."

"Then tell me something, man! Tell me something I need to hear to...to let you go. To let you...run." Walid's heart broke inside as he waited to hear something magical. "Please, brother. Can you fucking change?"

Ace saw the pain written all on his face.

In his eyes.

Walid could fake for the world, but he knew at that moment that he loved him, and that it was going to be the hardest thing he ever had to do. To take his life.

So he was done fighting.

Ace looked back at the car where Arbella sat. Then he looked at his brother. "I ain't got nothing, man. And that's for real. Because you and I both know that even though pops would be good if I survived, father will never let me live. And if I can't live, I mean *really* live, then I wanna die."

Walid was crushed.

"I want you to take care of my son," Ace continued, moving closer. "He's at the brothel in

250   **By T. STYLES**

the states. Aliyah knows the place." He paused. "I don't want him on the outskirts like me. I want...I want you to raise him as your own. And if you want to, only if you want when he comes of age, tell him of this moment. And how I wished for his happiness and peace."

Ace crushed him harder.

Walid was wrecked. His eyes blurred with hard tears.

"Can you promise me you will love him like your own?" Ace pressed harder. "Say it! I need to hear the words!"

"I will...I will raise him and my son like they are..." A sob pushed out of his soul. "...like they are brothers."

Slowly, Ace walked over to the vehicle where Arbella sat inside and opened the door. Yazo and the gang were still ready for whatever.

"This is it," he said to her, wiping her hair behind her ear. "And I want you to know that I have never loved anybody like I love you. And even though it was short lived if I had it to do over I would do it all again. Just to be with you."

"Ace...I...my...God please don't leave me. If you gotta die please tell them to take me too. Please."

He kissed her trembling hands and kissed her passionately on the lips. Then he let her go.

"I will look for you in hell, my Arbella."

"Then it won't be long," she sniffled.

Walking up to Walid he snatched the gun out of his hand.

Walid's eyes widened as he stepped back.

"Fuck is you doing?" Yazo asked, with wild crazy eyes waiting on Walid's word to blast him. "He's gonna—."

POW!

Ace's body dropped.

To save his brother's soul, he took his own life with a bullet to the heart. Walid hit the ground and gripped his twin in his arms, just as he took his last breath. Pain like he couldn't envision came out in the form of tears. This hurt more than he ever imagined, and he was glad he took the ordeal from Mason because he wished this on no one.

On the ground, he waited until he was ready to release his twin.

Waited until he was ready to let him go.

And when he was certain he would not be returning this lifetime, quickly, covered in his brother's blood he walked stiffly up to the van. At this point anybody could get it, especially that bitch. His eyes were lifeless and with his twin's death, he would never be the same.

"Listen up, bitch, can you be a mother to my brother's son or nah?" He had to know right here and right now.

Arbella was wrecked as she held her stomach upon seeing Ace's body outside on the ground. "He's gone." She sobbed. "Oh my God, he's gone!"

"ANSWER THE MOTHAFUCKIN' QUESTION!"

Wiping the tears away from her eyes she raised her head and said, "Fuck that little nig—." Walid shot her in the chest and watched her slump to the side before she finished her disrespect.

In that fateful moment, Ace's legacy was done leaving pain and heartbreak in its path.

In the pitch-black confines of the suite, Banks was seated on the sofa. He had gotten the news that his son was dead and even though the hotel held him captive, he wanted a few hours alone within its walls.

Now he was ready for someone else to pay.

With the window open allowing just enough light for Paulo to see him as his guard forcefully brought him inside, he waited. Banks' man closed the door and remained inside.

"Have a seat," Banks said.

"Sir, I want you to know that I didn't mean to hurt you or your children. I just–."

"Sit down. At the desk."

The air was heavy, and a dark energy took over the room, casting long shadows that danced across the walls.

He took his seat.

Banks rose and stood next to him.

"I warned you." His voice cut through the darkness like a razor. "I told you I would win. And you didn't believe me. Do you believe me now?"

He reminded Paulo of the evil he had inflicted upon his adult children, the pain he had inflicted upon their lives within the corridors of that hotel. Each word dripped with venom, echoing in the stillness of the night.

"I'm going to do more for you than what you did for my family." Banks, a shadowy figure, exuded an aura of vengeance. "Write a letter to your children." He reached into the desk and handed him a pad and a pen.

254   By T. STYLES

"Sir, please don't do–."

"Write, nigga! I won't say it again!"

He complied.

The harsh scratching of a pen against paper filled the air. Each stroke felt to Paulo like it could be his last word. Paulo's trembling hand felt heavy as tears rolled down his face. When he was done, he looked at the pen. It was the one Banks said he didn't have.

"So you kept it after all." He looked up at him, tears in his eyes.

"Fuck you think, nigga."

Banks took it from his hand, smiled and jammed it in the side of his throat. He watched as blood spurted from his vein before he walked out the door.

EPILOGUE

Months had passed since the climactic events that had unfolded in Belize, and the Wales and Louisville family had journeyed to the comforts of their new opulent mansion in the States.

Within the confines of their grand home, secrets and uncertainties continued to simmer beneath the surface, threatening to unravel the fragile peace they had fought so hard to reclaim after Ace's demise.

Blakeslee, carrying a secret of her own, found herself battling with the weight of an unspoken truth. Hidden beneath her composed fake smile, she carried the precious gift of new life within her growing belly.

She was pregnant with Mason's child.

This was some bullshit!

Fear and anticipation mingled within her as she sought to shield her pregnancy from the prying eyes of Mason and Banks, unsure of the ramifications such news would bring to the family.

After all, Mason was clear.

No Banks...no them.

And so, as they continued their lovemaking in secret, a baby could destroy it all. And yet she had no plans to give it up. Besides, Minnesota had stolen her last baby and this one would be her own.

And then there was Twin.

Walid, burdened by the weight of the irreversible act he committed, became dark inside. The haunting memory of his brother's life being extinguished in front of him echoed through his thoughts, yielding a shadow over his every waking moment.

The struggle to reconcile the conflicting emotions within him threatened to consume him, leaving him feeling like an imposter. It didn't help that Mason and Banks kept asking if he was okay. Kept asking if he needed anything. When in all honesty he needed to be left alone.

Well, almost alone.

A different woman kept his bed every few days and that was not an exaggeration. Distraction was the only thing that seemed to work. And so he partook of the pussy often. Although consumed with jealousy, Aliyah rushed over every day, and took care of him. Cooked for him, even as she bypassed women entering and leaving his bedroom. He belonged to her, and she would wait for him to come to that realization.

One thing that Walid liked was how she treated his brother's son. She did well by Roman and since he already knew her, the bond growing between Roman and Baltimore was concrete.

Walid was keeping his promise.

Meanwhile, Minnesota, Spacey, and Joey, forever bonded by their shared ordeal, found peace in one another's company. They became a weird ass clique who would talk in the shadows while isolating themselves from family.

If Minnesota wasn't with Sugar, raising her and loving her, she was with her brothers and she preferred it that way.

The New Triad is what folks called them.

Banks spoke very little about his wife, Faye, being killed.

It was embarrassing anyway. Why hadn't he known she was treacherous?

So after learning she helped Ace dig into his accounts, he figured she put the nail into her own coffin.

Good riddance!

And now it was old friends time.

By T. STYLES

Mason walked into the grand lounge of their mansion and found Banks sitting in a plush chocolate armchair, a glass of whiskey in his hand, the amber liquid swirling within. The room was filled with a subtle aroma of aged wood and rich leather, the way they both liked it.

"Got any for me?"

"Always," Banks said.

Taking a deep breath, Mason approached his friend, poured himself a glass and sat in his armchair to Banks' right.

"Banks," Mason began, his voice filled with nervousness. "I need to talk to you about something... something important." He took a deep sip.

Banks glanced over from his whiskey glass, his gaze meeting Mason's troubled eyes. Taking a sip of his drink, he gestured for Mason to continue. "I'm listening."

Hesitant, Mason's words stumbled outward. "I... I need to tell you something. It's about Blakeslee."

Banks' eyes narrowed slightly. "You want to talk to me about my daughter? Is that what you choose to do right now?" His gaze lowered.

Mason swallowed.

Did he already know but choose not to hear the details?

Instead of the truth he said, "How you two holding up?"

Banks let out an audible sigh. And Mason felt relieved.

"We're in a space," he took another sip. "A weird space. That's all I can say. For now."

Mason nodded and drank his entire glass. "How you holding up? With Ace... being gone?" He was hoping to gauge his friend's emotional state before revealing his own transgression.

Banks took a moment to collect his thoughts. With a sigh, he raised his glass to his lips, taking a slow, contemplative sip. "As long as the rest of the family is safe, I could care less about that nigga," his voice held a touch of rage. "Ace's actions brought us to destruction, and his demise, tragic as it may be, put me at ease. In other words, I'm sleeping good at night."

Mason didn't feel the same.

Walid either.

Then again, Banks was one of a kind.

Mason absorbed Banks' admission. He realized that this was not the moment to confess his own indiscretions, as Banks was struggling with rage.

260

And so, they shared a moment of silence as they both sipped their whiskey, the weight of the future on their shoulders. First Ace was dead, second Walid saw it go down and third they were back in America, a place they said they'd never return.

Where enemies still lurked.

Anything could happen.

Anything had happened.

And as the two friends sipped their liquor, they felt confident they could deal with whatever.

At least Mason hoped.

By T. STYLES

CARTEL PUBLICATIONS

PRESENTS

The Cartel Publications Order Form

www.thecartelpublications.com

Inmates **ONLY** receive novels for $12.00 per book **PLUS** shipping fee **PER BOOK.**

(Mail Order **MUST** come from inmate directly to receive discount)

Shyt List 1	_____	$15.00
Shyt List 2	_____	$15.00
Shyt List 3	_____	$15.00
Shyt List 4	_____	$15.00
Shyt List 5	_____	$15.00
Shyt List 6	_____	$15.00
Pitbulls In A Skirt	_____	$15.00
Pitbulls In A Skirt 2	_____	$15.00
Pitbulls In A Skirt 3	_____	$15.00
Pitbulls In A Skirt 4	_____	$15.00
Pitbulls In A Skirt 5	_____	$15.00
Victoria's Secret	_____	$15.00
Poison 1	_____	$15.00
Poison 2	_____	$15.00
Hell Razor Honeys	_____	$15.00
Hell Razor Honeys 2	_____	$15.00
A Hustler's Son	_____	$15.00
A Hustler's Son 2	_____	$15.00
Black and Ugly	_____	$15.00
Black and Ugly As Ever	_____	$15.00
Ms Wayne & The Queens of DC **(LGBTQ+)**	_____	$15.00
Black And The Ugliest	_____	$15.00
Year Of The Crackmom	_____	$15.00
Deadheads	_____	$15.00
The Face That Launched A Thousand Bullets	_____	$15.00
The Unusual Suspects	_____	$15.00
Paid In Blood	_____	$15.00
Raunchy	_____	$15.00
Raunchy 2	_____	$15.00
Raunchy 3	_____	$15.00
Mad Maxxx (4th Book Raunchy Series)	_____	$15.00
Quita's Dayscare Center	_____	$15.00
Quita's Dayscare Center 2	_____	$15.00
Pretty Kings	_____	$15.00
Pretty Kings 2	_____	$15.00
Pretty Kings 3	_____	$15.00
Pretty Kings 4	_____	$15.00
Silence Of The Nine	_____	$15.00
Silence Of The Nine 2	_____	$15.00

Silence Of The Nine 3		$15.00
Prison Throne		$15.00
Drunk & Hot Girls		$15.00
Hersband Material **(LGBTQ+)**		$15.00
The End: How To Write A		$15.00
Bestselling Novel In 30 Days (Non-Fiction Guide)		
Upscale Kittens		$15.00
Wake & Bake Boys		$15.00
Young & Dumb		$15.00
Young & Dumb 2: Vyce's Getback		$15.00
Tranny 911 **(LGBTQ+)**		$15.00
Tranny 911: Dixie's Rise **(LGBTQ+)**		$15.00
First Comes Love, Then Comes Murder		$15.00
Luxury Tax		$15.00
The Lying King		$15.00
Crazy Kind Of Love		$15.00
Goon		$15.00
And They Call Me God		$15.00
The Ungrateful Bastards		$15.00
Lipstick Dom **(LGBTQ+)**		$15.00
A School of Dolls **(LGBTQ+)**		$15.00
Hoetic Justice		$15.00
KALI: Raunchy Relived		$15.00
(5th Book in Raunchy Series)		
Skeezers		$15.00
Skeezers 2		$15.00
You Kissed Me, Now I Own You		$15.00
Nefarious		$15.00
Redbone 3: The Rise of The Fold		$15.00
The Fold (4th Redbone Book)		$15.00
Clown Niggas		$15.00
The One You Shouldn't Trust		$15.00
The WHORE The Wind		
Blew My Way		$15.00
She Brings The Worst Kind		$15.00
The House That Crack Built		$15.00
The House That Crack Built 2		15.00
The House That Crack Built 3		$15.00
The House That Crack Built 4		$15.00
Level Up **(LGBTQ+)**		$15.00
Villains: It's Savage Season		$15.00
Gay For My Bae **(LGBTQ+)**		$15.00
War		$15.00
War 2: All Hell Breaks Loose		$15.00
War 3: The Land Of The Lou's		$15.00
War 4: Skull Island		$15.00
War 5: Karma		$15.00
War 6: Envy		$15.00
War 7: Pink Cotton		$15.00
Madjesty vs. Jayden (Novella)		$8.99
You Left Me No Choice		$15.00
Truce – A War Saga (War 8)		$15.00
Ask The Streets For Mercy		$15.00
Truce 2 (War 9)		$15.00
An Ace and Walid Very, Very Bad Christmas (War 10)		$15.00
Truce 3 – The Sins of The Fathers (War 11)		$15.00
Truce 4: The Finale (War 12)		$15.00
Treason		$20.00
Treason 2		$20.00
Hersband Material 2 **(LGBTQ+)**		$15.00
The Gods Of Everything Else (War 13)		$15.00

The Gods Of Everything Else 2 (War 14) _____ $15.00
Treason 3   _____ $15.99
An Ugly Girl's Diary   _____ $15.99
The Gods Of Everything Else 3 (War 15) _____ $15.99
An Ugly Girl's Diary 2   _____ $19.99
King Dom (LGBTQ+)   _____ $19.99
The Gods Of Everything Else 4 (War 16) _____ $19.99

(**Redbone 1 & 2** are **NOT** Cartel Publications novels and if **ordered** the cost
is **FULL** price of $16.00 **each plus shipping. No Exceptions**.)

Please add **$7.00** for shipping and handling fees for up to **(2) BOOKS
PER ORDER**. (INMATES INCLUDED) (See next page for details)

The Cartel Publications * P.O. BOX 486 OWINGS MILLS MD 21117

Name: _____

Address: _____

City/State: _____

Contact/Email: _____

Please allow 10-15 BUSINESS days Before shipping.

***PLEASE NOTE DUE TO <u>COVID-19</u> SOME ORDERS MAY TAKE UP TO <u>3 WEEKS</u>
<u>OR LONGER</u>
BEFORE THEY SHIP***

The Cartel Publications is <u>NOT</u> responsible for <u>Prison Orders</u> rejected!

<u>NO RETURNS and NO REFUNDS</u>
<u>NO PERSONAL CHECKS ACCEPTED</u>
<u>STAMPS NO LONGER ACCEPTED</u>